Edward Edwin Foot

The Original Poems of Edward Edwin Foot

Edward Edwin Foot

The Original Poems of Edward Edwin Foot

ISBN/EAN: 9783337401559

Printed in Europe, USA, Canada, Australia, Japan

Cover: Foto ©Andreas Hilbeck / pixelio.de

More available books at **www.hansebooks.com**

THE

ORIGINAL POEMS

OF

EDWARD EDWIN FOOT,

OF HER MAJESTY'S CUSTOMS, LONDON.

LONDON:

PUBLISHED BY THE AUTHOR.

1867.

PRINTED FOR THE AUTHOR,

BY CASSELL, PETTER, AND GALPIN, LUDGATE HILL,

LONDON, E.C.

THE POEMS

OF

EDWARD EDWIN FOOT,

MOST RESPECTFULLY DEDICATED, BY PERMISSION, TO

HENRY WILLIAM DOBELL, ESQ.,

Comptroller-General of Her Majesty's Customs, London,

BY

HIS MOST OBEDIENT AND OBLIGED SERVANT,

THE AUTHOR.

PREFACE.

The Author[*] of the present Volume, in tendering his sincere thanks to the gentlemen of Her Majesty's Customs,[†] and to his other numerous and kind patrons, who so liberally subscribed towards the publication of his little work, assures them that he is deeply sensible of his obligations to them for the almost uniform courtesy with which his solicitations were met; because (being perfectly conscious at the onset of his undertaking how necessary it was to prepare to subject himself to censure as well as approbation, and to arm himself with those indispensable virtues—patience, perseverance, endurance, and thankfulness, without which the attempt would have been futile, and being also aware that nothing but a favourable response to his appeal could possibly lead to the accomplishment of his object) the success which has attended his efforts is certainly far beyond what might have been expected by one in so humble and so obscure a position in life.

There is, however, one gentleman[‡] in particular

---

[*] A native of Ashburton, Devonshire.　　[†] To which he belongs.
[‡] Sir F. H. Doyle, Bart., Receiver-General of Her Majesty's Customs, &c.

to whom it is the Author's duty to be—if 'twere possible—more than grateful, for his generous condescension in permitting the manuscripts to be placed in his hands for perusal, and who—after surveying a portion of them—not only recommended the method of publication which was adopted, but gave effect to his advice by kindly becoming the first subscriber to the work—for the Author never would have presumed to publish these poems on his own personal estimation of whatever merit they may possess, so that unless such an impetus had been given to the project it is more than probable he never would have had the gratification of seeing them produced in their present form.

This the Author hopes will afford to his numerous subscribers, and to those in whose hands it may perchance happen to fall, a not unreasonable excuse for his having intruded himself into the unmerciful arena of poetical literature, and, perhaps, be the means of saving his little work—the product of his leisure hours—from being thrust into the gloomy recesses of oblivion.

E. E. FOOT.

London, December, 1867.

The Poems of Edward Edwin Foot.

PUBLISHED 1867.

— ◆ —

CONTENTS OF VOLUME.

THE POEMS

OF

EDWARD EDWIN FOOT.

𝔄 Voice from the People.

[Composed on the occasion of the inauguration of the memorial statue of His
late Royal Highness the Prince Consort, at Aberdeen, 13th October, 1863.]

HAIL! virtuous Lady, England's pride ;
Abate thy grief, and gently glide
Among thy people, who—so free—
Have long'd thy widow'd face to see
Bedeck'd with smiles, and thou again
Enjoying tranquilly thy reign.
Come, Lady, and sweet comfort find ;
Come with thy children 'round thee twin'd,
For they shall reap that earthly bliss
Sown in thy former happiness.
We've miss'd thee, seemingly, for years ;
The while thou'st shed a nation's tears
For thine, for ours, for God's elect :
Come forth, conjointly to erect
Our heads, and give Him praise for all.
  Let Hope's bright rays again thy soul,
And ours, abundantly rejoice !—

B

That all thy subjects, with one voice,
May sing "God save our gracious Queen :"—
" Long live our dear and noble Queen
Victoria ;" who at Aberdeen,
To-day, amidst her people's seen
Unveiling to her country's gaze
A lov'd one's statue, ne'er t' erase
'T from memory.   With fortitude
The ceremony she withstood,
And taught the world how much she loved
The one whom she had so well proved
A husband, and a worthy sire,—
Once mortal ; now, immortal, higher !

   From thy deep solitude come forth
And tread the land which gave thee birth
With footsteps light ; thus, cheerily,
List to our songs so merrily
As thou wert wont in days of yore :
Come, be as blithe as heretofore,
Among thy people ; for we fain
Would see thy queenly smiles again.*

---

  * The author having sent a copy of this poem to Her Royal Highness the Princess of Wales then at Sandringham', had the pleasure of receiving the following letter :—

                          " Sandringham, November 4, 1863.

    " Sir,—I am desired to inform you that, by the direction of the Princess of Wales, I have to-day forwarded to Sir Charles Phipps, for presentation to Her Majesty the Queen, your poem, written on the occasion of the inauguration of the memorial statue of the Prince Consort, at Aberdeen. Her Royal Highness also desires me to say that she read the lines with great gratification.   " I am, sir,

                    " Your most obedient servant,

    " Mr. E. E. Foot,   (Signed)   " HERBERT FISHER.
  " 105, Ebury St., Pimlico."

O! Gather in the Old Yule Log.

O! GATHER in the old yule log,
　　No longer green and strong
In the forest of his ancestors,
　　Cheering the storm-blast's song;
Nor bending his oaken branches
　　In rev'rence to the gale,
Whilst echoing forth the forest glee
　　So hearty and so hale.

O! gather in the old yule log,
　　Whose lineage and renown
Bespeak for him a welcoming—
　　Such as is only known
In England's halls and palaces;
　　So trim him fair and neat,
And wheel him to the old recess,
　　Where he shall glow with heat.

O! gather in the old yule log,
　　The hall-door open wide,
And cheer his venerable corpse,
　　The forest's latest pride:
Yet whilst he's passing—ponder ye
　　O'er God's majestic ways;
For in him, gently gliding 'long,
　　There counts two centuries!

O ! gather in the old yule log,
   And range him on the hearth ;
No subject in the woodland glen
   Can tell of better birth.
Where is the heart not grieving (say ?)
   To part with this old friend,
That's doomed to blazon here to-night,—
   Two hundred years to end ?

O ! gather in the old yule log,
   Who rear'd his branches high
In the sunbeams of a summer's eve,—
   Heav'n's radiant canopy :
While waving in th' horizon, then,
   Ah ! then he could proclaim
His anger to the whirlwind ; but,
   Alas ! it conquer'd him.

O ! gather in the old yule log ;—
   Those leaves are long since fled
Which last adorn'd his stately limbs,
   And crown'd his tow'ring head :—
O ! could we sing of "glory still
   Encircling his old frame ;"
But no !—the only thing survives
   Is his proud ancient name.

Evening.

WHAT gulfs and ridges mark that shaded line.
    Which banks the setting sun !—
The rugged path of life it doth define,
    When mortals have outspun
        Their "three-score-ten" of years.

The rural margin, form'd by gentle slopes,
    Here, there, a cot or farm,
Reveals, as 'twere, a store of heav'nly hopes
    Possessing such a charm—
        We shed our tribute tears.

Blest is the hoary head that can with joy
    Behold the beauteous sight
Of the retiring Orb,—'neath clouds, so coy,
    Fring'd with his golden light,
        Without recurring sighs !

Whose magisterial beams so oft doth paint
    In the unbounded Vast,
Such gorgeous pictures as forbid restraint
    Of gladness.   Will it last ?—
        Oh, no ! the moment flies.

The city's margin of this evening scene
    Is form'd by spires, and domes,
Uneven roofs of dwellings ; where, within,
    The wearied find their homes
        In reeking atmosphere.

Yon tow'ring dome,* crown'd with a golden cross,
　　Not seemingly content
With its proud quantum of the ariel-moss,†
　　Still higher hath intent ;
　　　　But stay—this is thy sphere.

Beneath that sacred edifice, so grand,
　　There rests the dust of men—
Brave warriors, statesmen, and that skilful hand
　　Which wrought the fabric—Wren.
　　　　Ah ! 'tis a solemn sight.

The evening breezes bade the mist begone
　　From off this monument,　　·
Rais'd unto God !—then, in full glory, shone
　　The holy firmament,
　　　　So beautiful and bright.

Haste, haste, ye mortals,—lovingly behold
　　The goodly visitor !—‡
Another day is spent, and with it told
　　The last, the last !—sigh for　 *　*　*
　　　　But 'tis in vain—'tis fled.

Yes, yes, 'tis fled ; and with it gone for ever—
　　Forth from the mortal cave—
Ten thousand spirits to their first great Giver—
　　To Him, who Godlike gave :
　　　　But, Sol, thou art not dead !

---

* The dome of St. Paul's Cathedral, London.
† Dew.　　‡ The setting sun.

Those eyes that twinkle 'neath the grey-hair'd brow
　Of One with wondrous mind—
Defining laws to nations—teaching how
　Rulers should rule to find
　　Love in the multitude—

When clos'd for e'er, ah ! then thy country 'll shed,
　O ! generous Palmerston,—
Its tears for thee, and mourn that thou art dead,—
　And History shall mention
　　Thee,—in gratitude.*

The Homeward-bound Passenger Ship.

REFULGENT 'rose day's harbinger,
　And lit with joy the azure space ;
The good ship glided gently o'er
　The ocean's undulating face :

And on she goes, she ploughs the deep
　With seeming skilfulness and love ;
Her inmates gather out from sleep,—
　Some send their orisons above :

* The Author had the gratification of receiving a present from the late Viscount Palmerston (January, 1864), in acknowledgment of a manuscript copy of this poem.

While others,—thoughtless of the hour,
  When it is meet to bend the knee,—
Begarb themselves, display their pow'r,
  And revel on, as yesterday.

The cabin deck-light pane is bright,
  Which tells them 'tis a cheery morn;
(They do not dream—that ere 'tis night,
  Not even one shall live to mourn!* * *)

Good Zephyrus* speeds the ship along,
  She heeds it—lovingly she bows;
The sailors raise their bowline-song,
  And smiles adorn their iron brows.

All's well, and everything goes meet;
  The fleecy clouds, in sport above,
Afford an ocean scene so sweet—
  It tempers friendship into love.

The decks are wash'd, the breakfast-meal
  Is past, the passengers look gay;
Some pace the quarter-deck, and feel
  Desirous to prolong their stay.

A few are lounging o'er the poop,
  To see the log-line, out or in;
While on the forecastle, 's a group,
  Perhaps discoursing on the scene.

Mid-ships—some little children, there,
  Dight the clean deck in playful mood;

* The west wind.

While mothers hail them to repair
  Below, to take their mid-day food.

So "pleased as Punch" away they run;
  On Bobby's back his brother rides;
Dear little Susan loves the fun,
  And laughs enough to split her sides.

'Tween-decks, are now in dinner-trim,
  The frugal meal is well pursued;
And not a cloud had yet made dim
  The deck-light pane, above them view'd.

Sol now hath reach'd his highest point,
  The captain marks its altitude;
The beauteous orb's full golden front
  Gives to the seaman—latitude.

The chart is traced, the captain smiles;
  The rippling wavelets fly apace;
And all is well; Time thus beguiles,
  For joy appears in every face.

The cabin-passengers partake
  Their sumptuous fare, unlimited;
Out flies the cork! they freely slake,
  And thus their meal is finished.

Down yonder hatchway, in the shade,
  The dice or cards are nimbly dealt;
While those who move them oft degrade
  Themselves by adding sin to guilt.

Whilst farther aft, in best of hope,
    A group* seem pompous o'er their gain;
They saffron liquid freely tope,
    And whisk the bottles in the main.

The miser counts his money o'er,
    Then locks again his little trunk:
The spendthrift, as the day before,
    Flies to the bottle and gets drunk.

Here, there is one hums out a tune;
    And there, another fain would sleep:
(They little think, ere morrow's noon
    All, all would have to plumb the deep.)

Young wives, with rosy faces, trip—
    Sing tunefully as they go by—
Towards the galley of the ship,
    To boil, to broil, to bake, or fry,

Some little dainty—eggs, or ham,
    An omelet, or such rarities
As tarts composed with currant-jam,
    In readiness towards their teas.

(Oh! had they known it was the last
    Their beaming eyes would ever see;
Oh, had they known this one repast,
    Preceded their eternity!—

---

* Perchance a party of lucky adventurers: such, for instance, as three or four fortunate diggers, who probably had worked as a company on some gold field in Australia, and were returning to their native country.

Oh ! had they known what sighs and sobs,
 What streams of tears would sadly flit,
What beating breasts, what aching throbs,
 And how the sturdiest brow would knit —

They would have stagger'd on the deck !
 They would have shudder'd at their fate !
Instead of tripping by so quick,
 Intent upon the dish or plate.

Yea —e'en the pen that writes it down,
 Doth falter at the dismal thought—
That ere the sun, which lovely shone,
 Had 'rose again, the wreck was wrought !)

But whilst within the galley, lo !—
 A rather sudden lurch 'tervenes,
A little spray hops o'er her prow,
 And all is not so well, it seems.

Nay, more : a gloom pervades the deck ;
 The air is cool ; the sky 's o'ercast ;
The ship's smooth course receives a check ;
 The sturdy seamen scale the mast.

The captain scans the ruffled zone,*
 And heeds the wind's increasing scope ;
He knows full well, and reckons on
 His seamanship, but God's his hope.

An angry-looking cloud appears,
 Extends, and fast obscures the sky ;

* A figurative expression, intended by the author to signify the horizon.

The timid, nay, the stout heart fears
  A storm 's approaching, that 'tis nigh.

The beautiful and sun-lit main,
  Which greeted all at early morn,
Is dight with sullen clouds, and rain ;
  (Already is a jib-sail torn.)

The whistling wind seems full of woe—
  The roy'l-top-gallant yard is broke ;
The boatswain calls aloud, " Let go !'"
  And ere another word is spoke,

A sea hath struck hard on her port ;*
  The gale increases fearfully ;
For safety now the crew resort,
  And fasten down the main-hatchway.

The first dread peal of thunder rolls ;
  And loud, and louder shrieks the wind ;
The captain, through his trumpet, calls—
  " Make fast the spanker-boom, behind."

" Ay, ay, sir," is the pert reply,
  As readily it is obey'd ;
While some below prepare to die
  On bended knee, with lifted head.

The sweating helmsmen try, in vain,
  To guide her through the troubled sea ;
And as she pitches in the main,
  They labour on incessantly.

* Port-bow.

Stripp'd of her gayest canvas clothes
  She seems undone, yet faileth not
(Though turbulently toss'd) like those
  Who to their sleeping berths have got.

She willingly doth brave the storm :
  But now the elements conspire,—
The lightning flits in hideous form,
  And tints the ship with ghostly fire !

The thunders clap with horrid din,
  The minute-guns their storm-cries send ;
The fearful shrieking hurricane
  Her foretop-gallant mast doth rend !

Sea after sea, leaps o'er her bows ;
  Sail after sail, are torn in shreds ;—
The angry trough more angry grows,
  And would-be sleepers fly their beds !

Confusion reigns above, below,—
  And Jews and Gentiles fear the Lord,—
Yea, strong men seem as children now,
  And strive to utter forth the word.*

The boats are lower'd in dreadful haste ;
  But 'tis too late,—for, one by one,
The merc'less ocean lays them waste ;
  And fruitless is the minute-gun.

At last the captain, in despair,
  Exhorts the passengers t' attend

* Prayer.

Unto his last few words of prayer,—
  To meet their 'nevitable end!

In every feature death is seen,
  In every gesture dire dismay,
For now the seas are stoving in
  The starboard, gunwale, and gangway.

For hours the pumps in vain were mann'd,
  As tenfold did the waters rise;
The pumpers frenzically scann'd * * *
  And some, unnerv'd, betear'd their eyes.

(My muse doth falter to go on,
  But on I must, so on I write,—
Though tears are all but trickling down,
  As I bewail that mournful night.)

Then mothers, with their infants, cry
  And pray, if ne'er before they pray'd;
And those that knew not how, now try:
  But in an instant all is said!—

The ship hath rent herself in twain:
  A hundred shrieks, and all is lost!
Now, now the furious raging main
  Engulfs the overwhelmèd host.

And not a single craft at hand
  To witness, or to render aid? * * *
(Read on, if thou canst understand
  The dreadful havoc that was made.)

The day before, the sailors' song
    Rang merrily upon the ear;
Sweet infants to their mothers clung,
    And fathers did their children cheer.   ˙

The night before, the mainmast-truck
    Strain'd lovingly the courter's eye;
Though lack'd it inland flowers to pluck,
    The spangled stars flow'rèd the sky.

The good moon took her wonted tour
    Along an almost cloudless sky;
Round roll'd the planets as of yore,
    And all was pleasant to the eye.

Yes, all was pleasant to the eye
    To see the myriad wavelets play,
Or frolic, as it were, so coy
    Upon the moon's expansive ray.

Ah! then she furrow'd the green sea,
    And toss'd the phosphorescent spray,
As on she glided merrily
    Along th' unfathomable way.

Next (as the muse described before)—
    Refulgent 'rose day's harbinger;
. A prosperous voyage seem'd in store
  . For passenger and mariner.

The Ocean donn'd its garb of green,
    And every little wave that rose

Enhanc'd the beauty of the scene;
   And here and there did birds repose.

They watch'd the vessel's onward course;
   The refuse crumbs to them were bliss:
Although its particles were coarse,—
   They peck, and deem'd it not amiss.

(Oh! would that vessel 'd been a bird,
   To 've flown beyond the gale's dread scope.
And then to've dropp'd again unheard,
   Again sail'd on with former hope.)

They saw the ship, dismantled, sink,
   And 'lighted on the floating wreck :—
Yea, on the whirlpool's ghastly brink,
   They mock'd the dying on the deck,

(Saw they, alone, the craft divide—
   Save Him, in heaven, whose unknown way
Sets men's poor handiworks aside,
   And summons them t' eternity!)

And on the foaming billows lept
   With bird-like simile of joy;
Thereon they swung, thereon they slept.
   Until the next returning day.

Then, while the sun, swol'n round and red,
   Was garnishing the lolling sea,
Uprose the albatross and fed,
   (And fed, I ween, luxuriously.)—

Perch'd on a barrel, block, or spar,
　　An upset boat, a riven mast,
A rope, that shone afresh with tar,
　　Which yielded to th' unerring blast.

Or on, methinks, a sailor's trunk
　　(Ransack'd in haste for some lov'd thing),
The bottle which, perhaps, got drunk
　　Him who was last to laugh and sing,—

Unwilling to believe his soul
　　Would vanish with another breath,
Beyond the influence of the bowl,
　　Into th' eternal gulf of death !

(O God, forbid that such an one
　　Should breathe his last in such a state !
Or ever an unholy son
　　Inebriately should meet death's fate.)

Look, look ye down the plumbless deep,
　　See,* if ye can, their lifeless forms !—
Here laid, poor things ! across a steep,
　　An infant in its mother's arms ;

There, it may be, a man and wife
　　(Embracing either now as when
They went to rest at night, in life),
　　Are resting in a turbid glen ;

And here a damsel, once so fair,
　　A smile still lurking on her cheek,

* Imagine.

C

. But now across that cheek her hair
    Is floating wildly in a creek ;

There, laid a stripling, great in build,
    A leathern girdle 's round his loins,
In which a pocket 's nearly fill'd
    With sundry gold and silver coins.

Oh ! could we see the ocean's bed,
    (Strewn o'er, no doubt, with mangled bones,
And where there are no bones, instead
    Lie gems of rare and precious stones—

Jewels of value set in gold,
    And gold engraved by skilful hands,
With marks of friendship on them told,
    Near 'bliterated by the sands,)

Our sorrow would vent out in tears ;
    Nay, should we not, think, shun the sight,—
To see more than a thousand years
    Of dismal relics prone to light ? *   *   *

Now in the morn, when all was o'er,
    And heaven reveal'd the glorious sun—
When the dire tempest roar'd no more,
    And all those leaden clouds were gone—

It chanc'd the ocean's limpid breast
    Bore on and on a minor craft,
From head to foot garb'd in her best,
    And meetly trimm'd afore and aft.

Observant did her seamen see
   (What prov'd, indeed, too true a sign !)
A splinter'd wreck of the *Dundee* —
   (Ah ! once a " clipper " of the " line ")—

On which they read the name in full,
   And grasp'd it as it hugg'd the side ;
For then the zephyrs seem'd to lull
   Expressly to obey the tide.

This cast a sudden gloom on board,
   A sort of stupor seiz'd the crew ;
They solv'd the mystery in a word—
   She's lost !   Then farther on they view

The drifting particles of woe,
   Strewn o'er the now peace-waving main.
Confirming what they sadly knew—
   " That she would never sail again ! "

"Raven Rock." *

SOME summer's day, upon that rock—
A cliff, wherein the ravens flock,
    List ye to the Dart,† below ;
    See the little rapids flow :—
From that proud stream no discords rise
No shipwrecks e'er bedim our eyes.

Oft have I‡ watch'd, thereon, its course,
(Astride the rock, as 'twere a horse,)
    Singing o'er a favourite song,
    Twice and thrice to make it long ;
Then closed my ears against the stream,
And fancied that it was a dream.

But when I open'd them again,
I heard the same harmonious strain,—
    Saw the river stickling forth—
    Hurrying southward from the north,—
And almost wish'd myself a wave,
As peacefully going to my grave !

---

* "Raven Rock" is about 500 feet above, and near the banks of, the river Dart : is distant about two and a-half miles from Ashburton, Devonshire, and bounded on the north side by Aswell Woods, from which easily accessible

† The Dart river, whose source is in the forest of Dartmoor, is most appropriately called the "English Rhine." The scenery in the locality of "Raven Rock" is very beautiful.

‡ The author of the poem.

On yon domain, surnamed the "Chase,"
And from the bank five furlongs' space,
    Standing in a pleasant spot,
      'Rises gentle Bouchier's* cot,—
Directed, east, towards a vale ;
And west, beshelter'd from the gale.

From this rude cluster,† miles away,
Hills, dells, and woodlands greet the eye ;
    None can prize it, as it should,
      'Less upon the rock they've stood :
To the right a mountain tow'reth,
To the left a valley low'reth.

Ah ! beauteous Dart, thou art a home—
In thee a myriad fishes roam ;
    Some, ensnared, are flung on high,
      Others revel 'til they die ;
And come what may, there is no sorrow,
And no preparing for to-morrow.

Behold a sea of lofty trees—
See how they gently heed the breeze—
    Sturdy-branching, skyward oaks,
      Fated for the woodman's strokes,
For thousands then were doom'd to fall,—
The knight's commands were "one and all."‡

* Sir Bouchier Wrey, Bart., the lord of the manor ; great in stature, and a most amiable gentleman.
† The rock.
‡ Thousands of rare oaks which embellished this beautiful locality, belonging to Sir Bouchier, were hewn down some few years since, to the great regret of the people of the neighbourhood.

Methinks I hear the axe, and saw,
Re-echoing through the wood below ;
　　　And the fell-man's clam'ring tongue
　　　Timing forth a welkin-song,
Whilst he obeys the knight's decree,
And labours on right cheerfully.

Now, Time, the ablest workman there,
'll lay the forest bleak and bare.—
　　　Listen to the crackling sound,
　　　As they topple to the ground ;
And where, like antler'd deer asleep,
They calmly lie upon the steep :

But not like them—to rise again
To grace the hillock, vale, or plain,
　　　Or bound the fence : for ever dead—
　　　Lopp'd and chopp'd from foot to head
Their limbs lie scatter'd o'er the ground,
Until the barker trims them round.

Ah ! never more will they o'ershade
The lovers' footsteps in the glade ;
　　　No : nor foxes, hares, or birds,
　　　Truant-playing flocks and herds,
Will evermore again be plighting—
Beneath their branches—love's delighting.

Some hoary oaks, far down the glen,
Have many a time half barr'd the sun ;
　　　When the clarionet gave note,

Followed by the piping flute,
The cornet, trumpet, and trombone,
The curling horn, and blurt bassoon ;

Whilst well-dress'd youths made virgin love,
And arm'd their sweethearts through the grove —
    Stealing from their lips a kiss—
    Paving paths to future bliss :
While old and young were there partaking
The blithe picnic's merry-making.

Hush ! listen :—fancy that you hear
The banging of the bottled beer ;
    Look, and see the sparkling glass,
    'Round the festive circle pass :
And then behold their smiling faces,
As some for frolic make grimaces.

Conceive the scene—a " country dance,"—
A granddame with a stripling, glance,—
    See them sweep the avenue,
    She 'n her new-made bonny blue :
Contrive your mind to hear their laughter,
As two-and-two they follow after :

Presume you see them flitting through ;
Return ; cross hands with I, or you ;
    Then posetting pair and pair,
    To the screaming fiddle's air,
Now halting step unto its tuning,
And then again their flight resuming :

Observe that happy little fellow,—
(Whilst those yon donkeys loudly bellow,
  'Mong the ferns close by the stream,)—
  How he loves the bread-and-cream :
His mother 'spies his pretty glances,
As she, with him— her husband—dances.

I've been again upon that rock—
A cliff, whereon the ravens flock,
  Listen'd to the Dart, below ;
  Seen the little rapids flow :
But I, alas ! saw not those trees
Which made such music in the breeze :

The knight's commands had laid them low ;
Not one escaped the woodman's blow :
  And that pleasant spot is bare
  (Save the coppice growing there),
Whereon so oft the violin
Had bade the merry dance begin.

Yet there remain'd a vast resource
Of holy-holly, bramble, gorse,
  Stalwart elms, and tow'ring pine,
  Chesnuts, and wild eglantine,
The maiden-ash, beech, whortle, larch,
Nut-blooming hazel, and low birch.

Full many a time I've heard the horn,
Along those devious pathways borne,
  When Sir Henry* swept the vale,

* Sir Henry Seale, Bart., of Dartmouth, Devon.

Reynard flew before the gale :—
Alas ! I know not why or how
Sir Henry doth not hunt there now.

Still (fancy leads my muse to dwell
On scenes I loved so truly well)
    Hear I now the hurried notes
    From o'er thirty chiming throats,
As when they bounded past those rocks,
A terror to the flying fox :

Close now my eyes, methinks I see
A hundred hunters there with me ;
    Horses, and their riders, standing
    On some spot of choice commanding ;
Whilst the fleet fox, awoke to day,
Stirs out to buckle for the fray.

I hear, as 'twere, the signal given ;
Espy the creature madly driven,
    Bounding off towards that Tor,*
    Where, perchance, he'd been before,
And where the knave directs his nose,
In hopes again t' evade his foes.

Oh ! tell me, tell me, Destiny—
Say, has the dark futurity
    Aught so joyous yet in store

---

* Buckland-beacon, a very high point, commanding an immense tract of magnificent scenery, and where there is a strong refuge for the hard-hunted animal.

As those little rapids' roar?—
Or e'en that lovely scenery
(Ere Bouchier sign'd that dread decree)

Which gladden'd oftentimes my soul?—
Or when I lifted friendship's bowl,
    With my comrades down the glen,
    Ere and after we were men;
Whilst the shrill trumpet, or the drum,
Desired the wanderers to come

To join the merry roundelay—
To make the most of the blithe day—
    While on high God's sun was bright?—
    (For after day must come the night).—
Ay! canst thou answer my request,
And give my longing temples rest? *   *   *

Alas! I fear, O Destiny,
The all unknown futurity
    Never will again impart,
    By that beauteous river Dart,
Or there upon those mossy rocks,
Where, where the cawing raven flocks,

To me (methinks) a hundredth share
Of pleasures I've partaken there:
    When full many a lovers' vow
    Were made, perhaps, and broken now—
Made and cemented with a kiss,
Resulting in, or not in, bliss.

Thus : some unto the altar led,
Have had to mourn a husband dead :—
    Husbands who so sprightly tript,
    Equally in turn have wept ;
And children of their parents 'reft,
Now orphans to the world are left !

But there are some, I hope, more blest
Than when they were the bidden guest :
    Turning to those scenes with pride—
    Where* he met his future bride ;
Or where her lover first she saw,
When saffron flushes mark'd her brow.

Since then—great changes have been wrought.
And many a thoughtless stripling taught
    How to praise, and who to praise,
    How to pass his Sabbath days ;
And many a maiden (mother now)
Have reverentially learnt to bow !

O Destiny, guide thou the hand,†
That once forsook his father-land,
    Vainly seeking after wealth,
    Instead of quietude and health,
And train his muse, that it may tell—
How sweet it is at home to dwell.

---

* For instance.
† A slight reference to the author's short sojourn in Australia, 1855-56.
⁎ A WORD FOR MY NATIVE PLACE.—Should any of my readers ever be making a tour to the west of England, I venture to say they will be highly gratified with the grandeur of the prospect afforded them on " Raven Rock," and other commanding points in that locality ; and there are several high Tors, besides other places of attraction, in the neighbourhood of ASH-BURTON, which will well repay the visitor.—E. E. FOOT, London, 1867.

" 𝕷𝖔𝖇𝖊𝖗𝖘' 𝕷𝖊𝖆𝖕."*

'Tis said two lovers (and it may be true),
　　For lack of reason, or of grace,
　　Lept from this rugged precipice
　　Down to the peaceful main below,
　　Whose silvery waters ever flow
(I'm more than glad it was not I or you).

Think ye, O reader,—while they scann'd the gulf,
　　What feelings must have rack'd their brain !
　　And picture in your mind the swain,
　　As forth he wandered through the grove,
　　Endeavouring to persuade his love. *　*　*
The thought, alone, is dreadful to one's self.

Dwell but a moment on the sorrowing scene :—
　　Her arms entwined around his neck—
　　His lips her orisons doth check—
　　And in this act they reel the clift ;
　　Another moment life is rift ! *　*　*
The ruffled waters are at peace again.

---

* " Lovers' Leap," which is situated in a very picturesque spot on the
banks of the river Dart, is a perpendicular rugged precipice, immediate y
contiguous to a carriage-road. Its summit is about seventy feet above the
river, and where, at the foot of the rock, the stilly waters flow ; distance from
Ashburton about three miles, and about half a mile from the foot of " Raven
Rock," which is seen on "Lovers' Leap" with great advantage.

What could, methinks, have caused such dread of life :
    Was it forbidden them to woo ?—
    And thus despairingly they grew,
    Till, mutually agreed, they swept
    The craggy brink, and overlept :
So, with the world, they finished all their strife.

Think of the sudden splashing of the stream,
    Which for a thousand years had flown
    Harmoniously careering on,
    Save when the clouds could not restrain
    Their burden from the moorland plain ;
And see each wave-ring's sun-reflected beam.

Now, as the waters 'gan again to smooth,
    A thousand little bubbles leap
    From up the bottom of the deep ;
    Say, what were these ? Oh ! globes of air—
    The breathings of the dying pair—
All telling mournfully the solemn truth.

Enough, enough : turn to a calmer day.
    Here, once, on issuing from the wood,
    The gentle Albert* stay'd and view'd. *   *   *
    The grandeur of the sight drew forth
    A plaudit of most precious worth
(For never did he more pass by that way).

* The late lamented Prince Consort, accompanied by the late Colone
Phipps, and two other gentlemen in attendance on His Royal Highness,
made a tour from Dartmouth, *viâ* Totnes, to Ashburton, and thence to
Tavistock *(en route* for Plymouth by this circuit', proceeding by way of the
river Dart, in the carriage-drive which passes over " Lovers' Leap," on the
20th of July, 1852 : Her Majesty Queen Victoria proceeding, in the meanwhile, in her yacht to Plymouth.

Turn'd 'round, he saw that midway pile,* wherein
    In safety dwells the black-wing'd fowl,
    While foxes 'neath them nightly prowl :
    And then he turned around anew,
    And bade the lovely spot adieu,
Expressing pleasure at the glorious scene.†

(But he, alas ! was in the harvest field
    Too soon ;‡ but God, who gave, received :
    Though it was hard for her who grieved—
    And never did one grieve more keen
    Than she, fair Albion's widow'd Queen,—
Taught the most earthly treasure thus to yield.)

The sun shone forth, and graced with golden strokes
    These time-carv'd crags, which intervenes
    Those various blooming evergreens—
    Dight here and there to garb the spot—
    That arch full many a cooling grot,
Succeeding waterfalls, and purling brooks.

The Prince sped on towards the moorland height
    ('Twixt ash, and fir, and oak, and pine,
    Fair attributes of England's " Rhine,"—
    The silver-beech, and gorse, and fern,
    Re-blooming every year in turn),
For Plymouth Sound must be regain'd ere night.

---

* " Raven Rock "—aspect south from " Lovers' Leap."
   † This is stated on the authority of Mr. G. Sparkes, of Ashburton, who had the honour of conducting His Royal Highness and suite through this part of the journey.
   ‡ Gathered to his fathers, December 14, 1861, in his forty-second year.

Through fragrant bow'rs, on, on the chariot hies ;
 Affrights, perchance, the timid hare ;
 Entraps the rabbit in the snare ;
 Sends high aloft the squirrel, too ;
 The pheasant, to its instinct true,
Spreads his fair sails, and to the azure flies.

" Ah!" some will say, " give me the open sea,
 A ' mackerel sky,' a gentle breeze —
 Much preferable to rocks and trees,
 And birds that build therein their nests—
 Give me the gull, that bravely breasts
The mountain-waves—these are the joys for me.

" Let me enjoy a ship's transporting sway,
 Replying to the faithful gale
 Which constant swells her trim white sail.
 I care not for the rock, the rill,
 The rugged precipice, nor dell,
Which landsmen praise and call fine scenery !"

But when the storm converges fiercely round—
 What say they when the ship is toss'd,
 Strikes, breaks asunder, and is lost !—
 Not one alive to tell the tale ! * * *
 Oh ! think ye 't better than the vale,
The ivied cluster, nook, or mossy mound ? * * *

No ! never, never be it sung or said—
 " Sea scenes can ever match the land,"
 Where, like to this, God's works so grand

Majestically dight its face ;
When Sol, empower'd afresh, with grace
Tips the lone cottage on the rough hill-side.

They're happy out at sea : I'm happy here :—
High on the moor, let me inhale
The beauteous waftings of the gale,
Or hear the mounting lark's blithe sound,
Reverb'rating the blue profound—
In the ethereal main, free from all care !

I long to roam about those woods, wild grown,
Where birds, at leisure, chirp so sweet,
And now and then like mortals meet,
Discussing instinctly their love,
And hatching little ones, which move,
Look up, are feather'd, wing'd, leap, and are flown

Like as their parents—full of joy and glee—
Out on the sun-tipp'd hazel hedge,
Or black-berried thorn, or myrtle, sedge :
Or bounding o'er the fallow plain,
In search of some incumbent grain.
"Tis true their life-time's short, but still 'tis free.

I love that precipice, of which my rhyme
Tries to depict unto the mind.
Go thither, thou 'lt be sure to find
(Though I might fail to pen aright)
A picture pleasing to the sight ;
And none, I ween, more fairer in our clime.

A Welcome to Alexandra.

[Composed on the occasion of the arrival of Her Royal Highness Princess
Alexandra, 7th March, 1863.]

* * * * *

AND London ope'd her portals wide;
 Her kingliest streets throughout were deck'd
 With love, and joy, and intellect,
To welcome forth the Danish bride—
  Fair Princess Alexandra.

She, one of Europe's daughters, meet,—
 Betroth'd to England's fairest son,—
 We hail'd! and hail'd as should be done!
In joy-clothes garb'd, we went to greet
  Fair Princess Alexandra.

She left her parents weepingly,—
 The parting gave her bosom pain,
 But hope re-cheer'd her o'er the main,
For Edward 'waited anxiously
  Fair Princess Alexandra.

With all the splendour could be shown,
 Her happiness we strove t' enhance;
 And when we caught her first bright glance,
Admir'd her as Britannia's own,—
  Fair Princess Alexandra.

Throughout the land, around the coast,
 The British heart lept lovingly;
 For on our eastward silvery sea,

A goodly ship bore safe its guest,—
    Fair Princess Alexandra.

When now the good ship came in view
    Gravesend, her banners waved on high,
    And shouts reverb'rated the sky,
As favouring zephyrs waft anew
    Fair Princess Alexandra.

Then every eye was stretch'd afar,
    And every tongue was tipp'd with bliss ;
    In every feature happiness :
All long'd to see proud Denmark's star—
    Fair Princess Alexandra.

She came ! the beauteous bride was met :
    Her royal lover sought her hand,
    And welcom'd her in Britons' land !
The host that saw can ne'er forget
    Fair Princess Alexandra.

Light as a fairy treads the bowers,
    And as an angel wings the sky,
    So, with her Edward, passed by—
Upon a sprinkling of sweet flowers—
    Fair Princess Alexandra.

The speedy trav'ler,* whizzing 'long
    As cautiously as tho' aware
    Whose lives depended on its care,

* Their Royal Highnesses, and the ladies and gentlemen in attendance, travelled by railway to London, where, at the Bricklayers' Arms Station, they were received by the Corporation of the City with great joy and magnificence.

Bore safely—in the royal throng—
    Fair Princess Alexandra.

The stately cortège wound its way;
    A thousand banners fann'd the air,
    And perfumes 'rose from ladies fair :
All London seem'd at holiday,
    For Princess Alexandra.

The City bountifully plann'd
    Its duties t'wards the stranger-child—
    Its commerce paus'd—and kindly smil'd,
And stretch'd its unmatch'd gen'rous hand,
    For Princess Alexandra.

From steeples high a thousand tongues—
    Whose joyous sounds speak far away
    The only tribute they can pay—
Peal'd forth their complimental songs
    For Princess Alexandra.

Westward* pass'd the cavalcade;
    Whilst music, in its happiest strain,
    Accompanied the gladsome train;
Ten thousand voices serenade
    Fair Princess Alexandra.

The clouds were wrestling with the sun :†
    Aloft their rev'rent tears were stay'd,
    Respectful to the virtuous maid;

* The route taken was over London Bridge, King William Street, Cheapside, by St. Paul's, Ludgate Hill, Fleet Street, Strand, Pall Mall, St. James's Street, Piccadilly, Hyde Park, Edgware Road, thence to Paddington.

† The morning was only partially fine. About half-past four o'clock it began to rain. The evening was very wet.

Then gently christen'd her our own—
    Fair Princess Alexandra !

The whizzing " trav'ler" sped again
    The fair enchantress of our isle,
    Unto that kingly domicile,*
Wherein awaited our bless'd Queen
    For Princess Alexandra.

The Castle gates with joy unfold ;
    The noble host their way did wend ;
    Fair Flora, Queen of Flowers, did send
Her perfumed rarities untold,
    For Princess Alexandra.

The grand old tower† smiled in the gale—
    As tho' it knew its hope had come—
    And seem'd to whisper, " Welcome home !—
Britannia's sons shall guard thee well,
    Fair Princess Alexandra !"

Night, graciously prolong'd the hour—
    In honour of its queenly guest,
    'Til Weariness demanded rest,
And beckon'd to her peaceful bow'r—
    Fair Princess Alexandra.

* Windsor Castle.   † The Round Tower.

A West-Countryman's Visit to London.

A CORNISHMAN, of some repute
　　Down where the good man dwelt,
Took thought, and courage into boot,—
　　At length so eager felt—
Set bravely out, at last, to see
　　What he could hear in "Town;" *
And, to repair his memory,
　　Took pen to scribble down
The marv'lous things he might espy.
　　Or aught that he might learn.
(This wisdom'd man, most verily,
　　Had mused o'er his return.)   *   *   *
'Tis said—that sixteen weeks, or more,
　　The plans had been devised
For Captain † Joseph's "foreign tour,"
　　And sixteen times revised—
Regarding his habiliment,
　　The quantity of cash—
The necessary complement,
　　To cut a Cornish dash.   *   *   *

Now, be it known, when Captain Joe
　　First plann'd it in his head

---

* London.

† "Captain" is a familiar term invariably applied to the manager of a mine.

NOTE.—This poem is, by kind permission, most respectfully inscribed to the Author's sincere friend, H. Caunter, Esq.

To go to London, half Westlooe *
    Determined he was mad :
Some said to him, " Insure your life—
    You'll sure to come to woe ;"
And others, " If I were your wife,
    I'd never let you go."
But " By the stars in heav'n," he said,
    " The man that tampers me
Shall have his passport to the dead,
    Besides his passage free."

    *   *   *   *   *   *

The first beam of th' eventful day
    Found Captain up betimes :
His wife persuaded him to pray,
    If 'twere but twenty lines :
And so he did (both kneeling down) ;
    But quickly after this,
Joe, like a boy, was up and gone
    Upon the road to bliss.†   *   *   *
Away they went—for she went too,
    To see him safely off ;
And whilst she's on the platform—lo !
    The engine 'gins to cough,‡
And cough, and cough ; and Joe, to see
    His dear, popp'd out his head—
Ejaculating, " God bless thee,"
    When (what ?) his hat had fled !

---

* Westlooe is a small town in Cornwall.
† Little dreaming of the sad disasters which were about to befall him.
‡ The puffing of the engine.

Of course, Joe bawl'd to get it back,
  The more he bawl'd he might—
For 'twixt the wheels it got a crack,
  Which smash'd it left and right:
His dear wife saw! and cried in vain,
  "D'ye see the mischief done?"
But onward steam'd the "Wicked Train,"
  And he, dear fellow, gone!

    *   *   *   *   *   *

So all the way to "London Town,"
  Bare-headed Joseph goes,
Save on his head the silken one
  On service to his nose.
Although possess'd of "means" whereby
  Another might be got,
Still Joe could not prevent a sigh
  On losing his best hat:
Yet cheerful, and apparently
  A king in his rough mode,
He pass'd the hours agreeably
  Upon the iron road,—
Took out his sandwiches and beer,
  And then would have a smoke,
Drew closer to a lady near,
  And (gravely) pass'd this joke—
"This fire-horse, ma'am, breathes very hard;
  I don't much like the brute;
We'd best, I think, be on our guard,"
  (She trembles head to foot,)
" For fear the beast should break his chains,
  And gallop off the line;

The devil seems to have the reins,
    And driving down some mine." *
  *   *   *   *   *   *
Then Captain wonder'd at the pace
    The hedgerows seem to fly ;
" The trees," says he, " appear to chase
    The clouds along the sky."
Again the sandwiches and beer
    Were called into request—
Such homely sandwiches, 'twas clear
    His wife had done her best—
But quite inadequate these were,
    Ere half the day was done ;
So when they arriv'd at Exeter,†
    He got a lad to run
Across the platform to the " inn," ‡
    To get a cake or bun,
A quartern of best " Plymouth gin,"
    And gave the boy a crown : §
But ere the lad came back again, ||
    The engine 'gan to " cough ;"
And when he felt the moving train
    Had really started off,
Joe curs'd and swore most terribly,
    Got in a dreadful rage :—
(The passengers who sat close by
    Attempted to assuage
The Captain's wrath, but 'twas in vain,
    He swore and curs'd the more.)

* Passing through a tunnel.
† Where the train stopped for ten minutes.
‡ The refreshment department at the station.   § A five-shilling piece.
‖ A very doubtful matter whether the lad ever did return.

At last, appeased, he slept, and then,
　Of course, his rage was o'er.
For many hours asleep he sat,—
　Until the sun went down,—
Then 'woke deficient of his hat,
　And also of his crown ;—
And, to his great astonishment,
　Arrived at the " great town,"
Where,* in his haste to get away,
　He tumbles o'er a trunk ! *　*　*
(Now, whilst he's down, he hears some say
　" The man is mad, or drunk.")
Springs up again, laughs out, "All right !"
　And bounds for Edgware Road,
Where (the first "public-house" in sight)
　Joe takes up his abode ;
Makes free with some refreshments, and
　Tells how his hat was lost ;
Remarks—the landlord's house was grand,
　And what the gas must cost,
And such-like things ; then goes to rest,
　But devil-a-bit could sleep,
For something saunter'd round his waist,
　Then lodged upon his hip　*　*　*
Fatigued, at last his eyelids close :—
　Thus, happy for a time,
He gets into a solid doze,
　And† mutters forth in rhyme—
" Where is my hat? where is my crown ?"
And, " Where, oh ! where is London Town ?"

---

　　* Paddington Station.　　　† In a dream.

(A gent—in bed adjoining him,
  In the same room—o'erheard
The purport of the Captain's dream—
  Remember'd every word.)

*   *   *   *   *   *

At length Joe rises, and prepares
  For the forthcoming day,
Fresh as a rose, and full of airs,—
  In sooth, quite prim and gay,
With the exception of a hat ;
  So he plung'd in the street,
Found out a shop, and righted that :
  Thus made himself complete—
Whilst, on his countenance, a smile
Told plainly how he prized his " tile."
  As this* was all Joe's broken cash,
    Nought better he desired,—
Quite good enough, he thought, to smash,
    And so, replete attired,
Went back and ordered breakfast in ;
    Reclined upon the chair ;
Made up his mind not to be mean,
    Now all seem'd—straight and fair. * * *
To breakfast ; but, so hearty, Joe
    Soon rang the bell again.
The waiter he came in tip-toe :
    Said Joe, in language plain—
" Dost thou call this a breakfast, John ?"
    (With a derisive laugh.)—

---

* Seven and sixpence—a singular coincidence.

" Bring in another steak well done ;
    For this I call but half * * *
No wonder Londoners look pale,
    And look so mighty thin,—
I s'pose ye chiefly live on ale,
    Or what ye sell for gin."
Obey'd, and satisfied to full,
    He 't once sought for his cash :
But lo—'twas gone !——a tedious lull :
    Joe's teeth began to clash.
He'd hair scarce none, tho' h' seem'd to have
    Abundance on his pate.*
Now, he exclaimed upon the knave ;
    Then, murmur'd o'er his fate.
(Oh ! 'twas a piteous sight to see
So brave a man in misery—
Confused, confounded, as was he.)
  *   *   *   *   *   *
With watch in hand, Joe 'gan to moan—
    While tears stole from his eye—
" Is this enough, John, as a loan ?"
    " Yes," was the man's reply.
"Ah ! John," said Captain, "this old jew'l
    Belong'd to my grandsire ;
To take it from me 'tis, 'tis cruel." * * *
    With cheeks flushed up like fire
The Captain rushed into the street—
    A labyrinth of beings—
In hopes somewhere a friend to meet.
    He scans all sorts of things,

---

* The sensation of one's hair standing erect.

And prays to Providence he may
  (His eyes bedimm'd with tears,)
Detect the rogue this very day :
  "That I might ring the ears
Of him, the wretch ! that plunder'd me,
  And brought me to such grief,—
Could I the rascal only see,
  'Twould be, O ! Lord, relief :
I'd thrust him madly in the muck,
  Him trundle to a toad :—
O ! heaven, pray change this direful luck,
  And let the devils goad" * * *
Joe almost swoon'd : he bent his head,
  And press'd his aching sides ;
A hundred times wish'd he was dead,
  And that d——'d rogue besides :
Search'd all his pockets o'er and o'er,
  But not a mite could find ;
Scratch'd his poor temples till so sore
  It worried his poor mind :—
Again he felt !—rais'd up his face !
  "What's this ? what's this ?" exclaim'd.
"A button ? no !—they're all in place,"—
  A "godsend !" ('tis reclaim'd).

*   *   *   *   *   *

Now in Joe's coat's abyss* had gone
  A fourp'ny silver piece ;
He found it, and a smile then shone ;
  He damp'd it with a kiss,

---

* Inside the skirt-lining of his coat.

And sought the nearest paper shop,*
    With pen and ink there drew,
Or wrote, or rudely tried to drop—
    A few lines to Westlooe,
And told his dear wife, " Agnes-Ann,"
    To send him by first post
Some money.   Thus the letter ran—
    " Dear Agnes-Ann,—I've lost,
I've lost, my dear, my leathern pouch,
    I've not a copper left;
I've been oblig'd to leave my watch
    To pay——, so do be swift."
(etc.)   *   *   *   *   *
  'Twas done : his wife took pen in hand
    And sent a " P.O.O.,"
To pay, she said, at "Saint-le-Grand,"
    Five pounds in gold to Joe.
*   *   *   *   *   *

The Captain not a friend could see
    To help him in this need,
So in the depths of misery,
    And dreadf'lly hungerèd,
He wander'd to and fro by day,
    By night he did the same,
And every now and then would pray,
    Until the letter came.—
Then Captain went to "Saint-le-Grand,"
    And found the " order " right,
And soon five sovereigns in his hand,—
    A welcome, welcome sight :

---

        * Stationer's shop.

Thought on his watch immediately,
 Intent, turn'd round to go
Back to the inn ; but suddenly
 Stopp'd short, and sighed ; for, lo !
He'd never thought (poor simple man)
 Of taking its address. * * *
So here was Captain Joe again
 Once more in great distress ;
In such distress of mind was he,
 He turn'd his eyes to earth,
And cried, " My watch ! " and instantly
 He curs'd his very birth.

Now recollecting Edgware Road,
 Joe thought if he went there
He might find out that grand abode—
 Where all seem'd " straight and fair."
Direct he goes ; and if in one
 Almost in every inn
Steps Joe, but could not find the John
 Who look'd so pale and thin.
So vex'd, indeed, was Captain now,
 That he resolv'd to go
And take the Train, and made this vow—
 " Ne'er more to leave Westlooe."
Throughout the journey he never smil'd,
 And sat as though in grief,
Breath'd not a sound to man nor child.
 Thought every one a thief. * * *
But there was one* look'd straight at Joe,
 Who thought it very strange

* The lady with whom the Captain joked on his journey to town.

That "only just a day or two
    Had wrought this wondrous change!"
Now (which augmented Captain's cares)
    He'd left at home the "lines"
Which told where liv'd those Londoners—
    Advent'rers in the mines.   * * *
Fast flew the train, and Joe got home,
    Where flock'd his friends to see
(As customary in the town),
    And list' attentively
To Captain Joseph's great account;
    But they were much surpris'd
To find he'd nothing to recount
    Save his being modernis'd;
For what Joe thought to have in store,*
    When first he started out,
Had vanish'd like a metaphor,
    And he† turn'd inside out.
*   *   *   *   *   *

Next day, as Captain "went to mine,"
    Alone, he did not care
How he his vengeance did combine
    With an alternate prayer;
Thus :—"Where is that long-cherish'd gem,
    That only legacy
My grandsire left me? Woe to him
    Who brought this misery!" * * *
That night poor Joe thought (in a dream)
    His watch might still be found,

---

* The Captain had promised his friends to give them a full account of his journey, &c., when he returned.
† His wit.

And when he 'woke retain'd the scheme,
  Resolv'd the plan was sound ;
Made up his mind what he should do,
  Arose and went forthwith
Upon his pony to Westlooe,
  There found out old John Smith
The Schoolmaster, and earnestly
  Urg'd him at once t' invent
A " vertisement," which cleverly
  To the " Great Town " was sent.
'T ran thus : " One night slept at an Inn,
  Near the Great West—— Railway,
A Cornishman, and then was seen
  At breakfast the next day,
In waistcoat, coat, and trowsers, black ;
  Who'd lost his leathern purse,
And left his watch : he wants it back,
  And would not care a curse
'Bout the expense if that kind Gent,
  Who took it for his bill,
Would pack it safe and have it sent
  Right down into Cornwáll,—
Address'd to Captain Joseph James,
  At Westlooe Copper Mine,—
And send his own address and names,
  With just a word or line,—
John Smith, of Westlooe Grammar School,
  Will send by the next mail,
In postage-stamps, the cost in full,
  And something for some ale." *   *   *.
This done, the Captain bade farewell,
  And trotted home with speed,—

Told his dear Agnes-Ann—the tale,
　　Took tea and went to bed;
And rose again, delighted with
　　The plan; then went to mine;
Thought all day long of old John Smith,
　　And of th' expected line
From "John" the Gent. At length there came
　　A note, wrote plain and neat,
Sign'd with a " Russian-looking name,"
　　At " 16, Cuthbert Street." *　*　*
Then Joe exclaimed, " My watch, my dear;
　　My dear, my watch :" and he,
To make her understand it clear,
　　Read out thus (smilingly)—
" If Captain Joseph James will send
　　In postage-stamps One pound,
His trouble shall be at an end;
　　The watch is safe and sound."
" Is safe and sound," quoth Joe thrice o'er;
　　"Oh ! thank the Lord for this,"
Said he; then read it through once more,
　　And gave his wife a kiss;
Put on his best, and trotted down
　　(The stamps got on the way)
To see his old friend " Maseter" John;
　　Shook hands, and 'gan to say—
" Dear Maseter John, once more I will
　　Just trouble you to write." *　*　*
" With pleasure, Captain ;" took his quill.
　　And penn'd with all his might
An answer to the honest sir,
　　Who saw the " vertisement ;"

E.

Enclosed the stamps, and sixpence o'er.*

* * * * * *

So great was Joe's content,
He went straight home and said his pray'rs;
 Became an alter'd man:
When bed-time 'rriv'd he went up-stairs,
 And bless'd dear Agnes-Ann.
Next morning like a lark he 'rose,
 And merrily tripp'd along
Towards the mine, and as he goes,
 Hums o'er his old lov'd song.

* * * * * *

Three days pass'd by: Joe doubted (what?)
 If all was strictly true;
And thought t' himself—hath "John" forgot
 Joe James of, of Westlooe? * * *
Another day pass'd o'er his head;
 His fears now 'gan t' increase;
He reckon'd up what he had paid,—
 The sum disturb'd his peace!
"Oh! sinner that I am," quoth he,
 "To put such faith in man;"
And paus'd: then bawl'd out savagely,
 "Oh! may the rogue be d——n'." * * *
Now, when poor Captain Joseph felt
 That watch and all was lost,
He grumbled something, sigh'd, and knelt,
 And counted up the cost,—
Which 'mounted to twelve sterling-pounds,
 Eight shillings, and odd pence!†

---

 * An extra sixpence to pay for a glass of grog.
 † Including the value of the watch, chain, &c.

Enough.   His anger knew no bounds,
   His rage became intense,
(With whom poor Captain Joe knew not)
   And e'en the beard he bore
He turn'd aside—aim'd at his throat !
   But failing this—he swore
That all but him * were rogues and thieves ;
   That every living soul,
From parish-paupers to state-chiefs,
   Would surely go to ————.

     *   *   *   *   *   *

" Come neighbours, drop a tear for Joe !"
   The sexton quaintly said,
When Captain Joseph was laid low
   Into his last lone bed.†
And so they did.   And even now
   Dull records prove the fact—
That never a man in all Westlooe
   Possess'd such mining tact
Before or since old Joseph died ;
   Or bore three prouder names—
If heav'n and earth were both allied—
   Than Captain Joseph James.‡

---

* The Captain himself.

† Grave.

‡ There seems to be no doubt whatever (assuming the story to be a true one) that the Captain's greatest disaster—his losing his old "leathern pouch," as he called it, occurred on the platform of the Paddington Station, when, in his great hurry to get away, he tumbled so violently over the trunk : and being in the habit of carrying his "pouch" in the inside breast-pocket of his coat, the probability is, that it escaped from thence in consequence of the sudden jerk it received.   He, as a matter of course, being a Cornishman, took very little—if indeed any—notice of the fall, for (with an air of triumph) he recovered his perpendicular, and started off—as observed before in the

England's Hope.

WHEN suddenly one wintry night,
Throughout the land with 'lectric flight,
    The news * sped far and wide,
Old England 'rose with sterling joy,
And hail'd the princely infant boy!—
    The offspring of our pride.

For whilst on Britain's favour'd soil,
Ten thousand round had ceas'd from toil,
    Kind nature rack'd her frame :
But Time, the god of hope and fear,
Deign'd not, in love, to linger there ;
    Relief was wrought and came !

And Providence, so wondrous kind,
Thus sooth'd a mother's anguish'd mind—
    The parent † of our hope :
Whose children's transient joys, or cares,
She most affectionately shares
    With gentle sovereign scope.

poem—in the direction of Edgware Road. As regards the disappointment
and dismay which the Captain met with afterwards as to the recovery of his
watch, that was what might have been expected by any shrewd person,
because it was very natural that some sharp individual would have observed
the "'vertisement," and would, as a matter of course, take some such a step
as, unfortunately for Joseph, turned out to be the case.

  * The accouchement of Her Royal Highness the Princess of Wales, and
the happy birth of a Prince, at Frogmore Lodge, Windsor, at 8.55 p.m.,
Friday, 8th January, 1864.

  † Her Majesty the Queen.

Thanks ! thanks ! a myriad hearts entreat ;
Look upwards and with zeal repeat
    This universal song,—
Grant to the mother, God, so good,
Thy daily gifts of choicest food ;
    And pour amid the throng,

On her Thy unction of sweet peace ;
Thy wisdom and Thy care increase,
    And save her from the foe
That robb'd us of a cherish'd name.*
Let health and charity inflame :—
    Command it to be so,

"Tis done !"   Praise, and with might implore
The righteous God, His gifts to store
    For the sweet infant prince ;—
To gird with strength and love combined ;
T' endow him with a generous mind :
    And let a people hence-

Forth render eagerly their arms,
If that false god—Delusion charms
    Or enemies incite
To dare invade the British Isles,
Our valour, hope, our tears and smiles,
    Shall guard them in the fight !

But may the warlike dream be this :
" A son receive a mother's kiss,—
    A father's fondness prove,—

* Albert. His late Royal Highness The Prince Consort died 14th Dec., 1861.

The only weapons to engage ;
The only conflict to assuage ;
    The only god—pure Love."

NOTE.—The author takes the opportunity of stating here that, having
sent copies of the three poems—" England's Hope," " Christening the
Prince," and " Our Little Brother "—to Their Royal Highnesses the Prince
and Princess of Wales as the three incidents occurred), he had the gratification of receiving on each occasion a letter expressing their thanks for the
same.

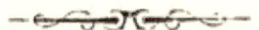

Christening the Prince.*

ONE circle round our Sun—and o'er—
Is perfected, since forth there stray'd†
In youth a fair Princess,
From whom fell liquid drops of love—
Love-crystals of her wedding tour.
Though griev'd, the fair-form'd gentle maid
(Whom God was pleas'd to bless),
With modest courage sweetly strove
And conquer'd it !—Joy helping her.
Those moments sad, Time soon spent out :
Her Edward, yet afar,
Beheld her with bright vision's eye.

    * The reader will please to observe that lines 1st and 5th, 2nd and 6th,
3rd and 7th, &c., have rhythmical terminations.
    † The author seeks indulgence in using the word " stray'd."

She wiped away the pearly tear,
And tripp'd on deck.   Then 'rose a shout
For Denmark's shooting star—
Resounding thro' the azure sky!
   Silently sped the ship over the sea :
   Edward beheld his Bride, happy and free.

England's store of wealth and fame
Burst forth in one united blaze,
And reel'd in ecstasy—
Love's civil war of Joy *v.* Joy !
To day, around the Font to name—'
(As on a courtly group we gaze
In seemly modesty)—
The pretty infant nursling boy,
A family of royal descent
Implore Great God's especial care,
For this, their lovely child.
   *   *   *   *   *   *

O bounteous Lord, who gave him breath !
Behold them reverently bent
Whilst offering up their pray'r
To Thee, Who kindly smiled :—
Defend and succour unto death.
   Now in their triple bond, safe from the sea,
   Edward beholds them both happy and free.

The Astronomer.

Cold, yet salubrious, is the night,
  And quiet reigns around ;
Mid-winter's nimbly spread its white
  Robe o'er the goodly ground.

The silver'd earth reflects the moon,
  As, in her majesty,
She rides across that vast saloon
  Where mystic meteors fly,—

Where giant stars,* all in their course,
  Roll through the plains of night,—
Sustain'd by their centrip'tal force,
  And centrifugal flight,—

Illuminating the blue main
  (Where discontents ne'er rise),
As on they travel in a train
  Through the enchanting skies.   *   *   *

Famed Venus, Jupiter, or Mars,
  Attract the passer-by ;
While countless other glittering stars
  Ne'er catch a single eye.

Some creatures, weary with their toil,
  Scarce lift their heads above ;

* The Planets.

And others, thoughtless of them all,
 Prefer their downs of love.

But the Astronomer's deep mind
 Soars through the ocean air,—
He loves the Hand which has design'd
 The heav'ns with so much care;

For in 't he finds a glorious feast
 Of beauteous wonderment!
Though thousands 'round him take their rest,
 He seeks the firmament :

Therein abides his only hope,
 And there his soul is lost !—
In solitude he loves to cope
 The grand nocturnal host;

His nourishment—the silv'ry draught,
 While 'tis a cloudless sky ;—
But lo ! he turns and views, abaft,
 Some striplings of dark dye.

And then a group, of murky hue,
 Seem to conspire to mar
The radiant twinklers from his view,
 And hide his favourite star.

All hope—awhile—now gone from him,
 He seeks his lonely bed,
And there he utters, in a dream,
 Those words—" When I am dead !" * * *

Awoke—his ever-studious mind
    Impels his feathery pen,.
And draws, perchance, his last design
    Of the ethereal main.

Ah ! something stirs him to a smile—
    Like lightning skips his quill ;
Then, for some reason, waits awhile,
    And sits, as 'twere, stark still :

Or, studiously obedient to
    The impulse of his heart,
Inclines his heavy-laden brow,
    And drops his grey-goose dart.

Then, when 'tis eve, he travels forth
    To scan the starry height,
With instruments of precious worth,
    And compasses the night.

Fix'd,* and directed to the spot—
    The object of his gaze—
Exclaims the man, " O, beauteous dot !—
    Some men, methinks, will praise

Thee more than I, when 'neath the sod
    My cold clay form is laid :—
When I th' immortal path have trod,
    They'll talk of him that's dead."   *

He strikes the bosom of his muse,
    And chants in silent song

---

* His astronomical instrument.

A hymn of joy, whilst he reviews
    The grand celestial throng.

He envies not the king his throne ;
    The nation its proud wealth :
But ponders o'er the purple zone,
    Till self-destroying health

Bids him relax the arduous task,—
    He sighs at every breath,—
For on his pale cheeks lurk the mask
    Of hungry-looking death.

Yet still assiduously goes on
    The man (not of this world) :
Until, alas ! his period's run—
    The sails of life are furl'd !

His worldly goods are sought by those
    The nearest of his kin ;—
On cumb'rous shelves, in cupboards, doze
    The products of his pen.

They see, at length, in their rude style
    That in the vast blue heav'n
There rangeth one more ariel-isle !
    Its name was all but given * * *

Enough though had been writ of it,
    Man's wisdom to absorb ;
For yet-liv'd 'stronomers deem'd fit
    To seek the new-born orb :—

Yes, and 'twas found ! and then they raise
A tribute to its fame,
And learn the dead man's works to praise.
And lauded forth his name.

———<o>———

.

On Shakespeare.

~~~

[Composed on the occasion of "The Shakespeare Tercentenary Festival,"
1864.]

HE liv'd to die, but not to be forgott'n,
Without a title save that his parents gave him,—
A proud yet simple one indeed,—
Such as almost a very babe might utter.
Although the dust of his birth-dwelling's long since
    trodd'n,
He's now, as was of yore, a glorious shining beam,
On which our memories love to feed.
His mother fondly watch'd his gentle stature :
Himself the womb of a rare sparkling brain :
And heaping, aye ! unthought of world-wide wondrous
    fame
With his enchanting pen :—the food,
The fondest food of history, and the stage :

NOTE.—The reader is requested to observe that lines 1—5, 2—6, 3—7,
4—8 (and so in every eight consecutive lines), have rhythmical terminations,
though the quantity of feet do not agree ; but the number of feet in lines
1—9, 2—10, 3—11, 4—12, 5—13, 6—14, 7—15, and 8—16 (and so in each
successive 16 lines), will be found to correspond, with but slight variation.

'Twas but a little cabinet that did contain
The ponderous manuscripts which bore his goodly
    name—
Those volumes so well understood.
O god of bards, thou wert the greatest sage !

   *   *   *   *   *   *

"The tempest" of life he did begin to fare
One April-month, 'tis writ (in Fifteen' sixty-four)
Not " much ado about nothing."
" Love's labour lost ?"   Oh, no—indeed 'twere not !
In him were planted tender shrubs, and striplings rare,
Which grew, at length, to giant trunks of strength and
    pow'r :
In literature he 'came a king.
To grasp the sceptre of the stage he wrote.

   *   *   *   *   *   *

Whilst but a youth, at Stratford-upon-Avon,
He stole, poor lad ! away from one Sir Thomas Lucy.
A lucky day was that for " Will,"—
When he began his " comedy of errors,"—
Startling, withal, men's minds for ever and anon !
Erst chalking satire on the knighted-man's own gate-
    way.
" Measure for measure," penn'd his quill,
And left poor Lucy, first to taste his terrors.

   *   *   *   *   *   *

O thou bright charmer of the inmost spark !
Why revell'd thou so soon in death's grim holiday—
Ere time had run its 'lotted space ?
In peace thy work began was finished well.
Like as the stars which shine throughout the dreary
    dark

Thy feather'd instruments made letters and words say
That thou didst live—didst live to chase
Gods to their heav'n ; and devils to their hell.

      *   *   *   *   *   *

(Men stirr'd themselves and ransack'd o'er their wit,
And did in their quiet homilies rack brain and soul
To render unto the great dead
A worthy tribute of their country's love.
With all the modern implements of learning writ
They—each and either of them—their own favourite
    roll :
" Not as you like it," be it said,—
He wrote a play while they their plans approve.)

" Will's" cloudy days nigh spent, his sun arose !
(God with him, tickling his fair brow and sparkling eye)
With wisdom wrote he 'n majesty
On high-born kings and lowly peasantry
In rhyme's sweet readings ; lines of quaint sarcastic
    prose :
Perhaps offendingly to some ; whilst others sigh,
Or laugh, or cry, and timidly
Enjoy the witty man's bright pleasantry.—
Behold his genius ! look ye to the skies ;
For like a planet, known by its respective sign,
So was he—good William Shakespeare—
Occupying the golden throne of history ;
Whose countless pages, fraught with gloomy mys-
    teries—
Stored o'er and o'er in ancient and in new design—
Are lasting monuments, so dear,
That he shall ne'er escape from memory.

The Banquet.*

THE summer crept from May to June,
    When flow'rs yield most their perfumes sweet,
And add their charms to the saloon,
    To make the banquet-room complete.

See : there they are, of every hue,
    Of every cast, in aspect rare ;
All greeting all who deign to view,
    And smiling on the happy pair.

Their meet companions all attend—
    Those crownèd giants of the pine,—
And in their place, beneath them, bend
    The goodly tenants of the vine.

Those purple cisterns,† fill'd to brim,
    (And those green beauties by their side,)
Enrich the little seas that swim
    In goblets, through the eventide.

'Round golden pedestals they cling,
    Among th' elect of every fruit :
Hear they, as 'twere, the glasses ting ;
    Burst they with joy, yet they are mute.

---

* This poem was composed on the occasion of the Banquet given by Lord
and Lady Palmerston, June 22nd, 1864, in honour of their Royal Highnesses
the Prince and Princess of Wales.
    Grapes.

Their turn is come—O, happy fate !—
   A kindly hand assists them down ;
They garnish well the polish'd plate,
   Until their fairy-life is flown.

Now listen to the harmony—
   Those compliments of courteous love :
Observe how wondrous loyally
   And royally the things do move !

The banquet-board bore on its face
   Profusion's burden of choice store :
The hostess loan'd her wonted grace—
   Enhanc'd by the gay garb she wore :

And by her side, on her right hand,
   The son of England's cherish'd Queen,—
Prince Edward, of all Britain's land :
   None fairer of his sex are seen.

Glance o'er the board—behold the host,
   (Whom this fair Prince doth honour well,)
Though years he numbereth the most,
   In wit and wisdom none excel :

On his right hand, eyes sparkling bright,
   Sat Alexandra, England's own.—
She saw, was seen, and spell'd the night :
   Yet there were other stars that shone,

Whose smiling countenances glowed
   With love, and hope, and charity ;
Within whose bosoms freely flowed
   The stream which mark'd their ancestry,—

Of ancestors who scared the foe
   With swords and bucklers, armour bent,
Swift arrows from well-bended bow,
   Or matchlock leaden bullets sent;

Whose loyalty unto the crown,
   When dangers frown'd at home, abroad,
Brought kingly gratulations down,
   And blessings from Almighty God.

Have ceased those feudal wars of yore,—
   When heritages were purloin'd,
Or purchas'd with death's clotted gore,
   To satisfy th' insatiate mind.

Now peace, triumphant, fill'd each heart;
   The rosy wine-cup teem'd with pride;
The banquetees* had met to part :—
   Gone, gone is this blithe eventide !

          * The guests.

Thought.

O SILENT tickler of the human brain !—
     The infant's, boyhood's, manhood's, and old age'—
In some thou 'bidest with consoling strain ;
     In others, burning with revengeful rage.

The babe is prompted to its mother's breast,
     While with sweet lullabys she heeds her child,
And dandles it, or rocks it on to rest ;
     Herself perchance a widow, or beguil'd :—

A widow ! and within her village cot,
     She sees the fence encircling the green sward,
And eyes the porchway, leading to the spot
     Where he lies mould'ring, once the village bard.

" Boys will be boys," and so they go a playing ;
     Methinks I see nigh twenty of them there
Who drop their marbling while the donkey's braying,
     And laugh most heartily at what they hear.

There, ten years hence, not one of them is seen,
     The field of industry absorbs them all ;
Yet there are others playing on that green,
     Knuckling at marbles, or at batting ball.

One well-known lad has gone across the sea,
     Another's crippled, and another's dead :
Out of those twenty there remains but three,
     And they have cares, for each of them have wed.

The man—a merchant, or a city-scribe,
    Has round him rang'd his family-group at night ;
His gains are great, and therefore doth subscribe
    Towards the evening's leisure of delight.

God's holy day comes round, they take in turn
    To fill the pew, for which he pays the rent :
They've not yet had occasion for to mourn,
    And so the intervals are cheerly spent.

He banks his cash day after day, perchance ;
    His sundry books are regularly pent ;
He speculates at home, in Belgium, or in France,
    For all goes well upon the Continent.

Speeds forth at morning in his usual health ;
    The family-group repeat their kind adieu ;
Once more he's on the path to gain and wealth,
    And meets a friend, who startles him anew !

The news of some disastrous incident
    Now smites him like a demon's evil dart—
The bank, in which he felt most confident,
    Is "broken," and will soon have broke his heart !

He then to Heaven uplifts his tearful eyes
    (Adversity had check'd the worldly spark) ;
Despairingly he ponders, then he sighs,
    Like as a seaman in a sinking barque.

Time, swiftly rolling, 'printeth on his cheek
    A hallow'd countenance, imbued with care ;

Once mighty,—humble, thankful now, and meek,
　And regular at morn' and evening pray'r.

Obedient to God's laws of life and death,
　Old Age prepares to meet Eternity !—
Deep furrows on his brow, and shorten'd breath,
　Are tokenings of his infirmity.

Recurs to him (when at his social board)—
　Some little element of jealousy,
Occasion'd through an inadvertent word
　Escaping, when in his prosperity.

He now repenteth of the injury done,
　And makes amends by words of lovingness ;
Calls to his side his dear and only son,
　Whose mind, refresh'd, at once forgiving is.

A thousand little things flit to his mind,
　With wondrous force of perspicuity ;
As in his old arm-chair he is reclined,
　Believes what once was incongruity.

The lessons of a life-time now hath taught
　The old man to put faith in holy things ;
He strikes his bosom, for a happy thought
　Revives some former truthful ponderings.

Alas ! he fails, bed-ridden ; (hence he dies.)—
　Some goodly creature reads the Book of fate.*
His family 'round him, sees him close his eyes ;
　And thus is finish'd the four-fold estate.

* The Bible.

Sheep.

How welcome 'tis to human eye
   To see the mead-lands gay with sheep :
How homely is the lambkin's cry ;
   How sweet to see them run and leap.

Look, whilst unheeded falls the show'r,
   How nimbly each one nips the blade ;
And, as the rain-drops trickle o'er
   Them, how intent they mind their trade.

Their life-time's short, but sweet content
   Ne'er fails them : on and on they pass,
And as they wander innocent-
   Ly yield, and aid the growing grass.

When Dame Aurora steeps the main
   With her resistless flood of light,
They're up, and at their trade again,
   And nibble, nibbling till 'tis night.

But when a storm is gathering fast,
   See how they'll seek some shelter'd cove ;
How cunningly they'll shun the blast,
   Beneath a hazel-hedge, or grove.

When down at night they gently lie,
   Unconscious where the light hath flown,
It may be plann'd for all to die
   Before the morrow's afternoon.

'Tis so !—a sound doth 'lectrify
   The timid throng : they congregate ;
And, as th' intruder they espy,
   Seem apprehensive of their fate.

Away unto some nook they run,
   Or to the angle of the field ;
The shepherd marks them one by one,
   And one by one they have to yield.

(Perchance it is the month of May) :
   Their shornèd quarters fat and fleet
Are needed in some other way,—
   Are soon, alas ! transform'd to meat.

O ! little faithfuls,—eat and drink,
   For on to-morrow you must fall :
'Tis good thou hast no thought to think ;
   Were 't so thy life-time would be gall.

Suppose it's March : the fields * are bare ;
   The hunter's horn rides on the gale ;
And suddenly a fox, or hare,
   Comes bounding over hedge or pale,

Then see them how they'll gather round,
   As though some dreadful foe was near ;
And mark, when forth the foremost hound
   Comes yelping onward, how they fear ;

And stand aghast-like—stark and still—
   Until the yelpers have flown past,

* Cornfields.

Until the hunters cross the hill,
   And then again seek their repast.

(Now when the distant sportsmen see
   The nervous flock haste to the fence,
'Tis known to them with accuracy
   The prey hath cross'd, or crossing thence.)

Ah! little think they (but 'tis true)
   That, as they heed the fleeting throng,
Those hunters' coats, red, green, or blue,
   Have from such backs as theirs been flung.

Turn, reader, from the blithesome chase
   To where the staggering thrust is dealt ;
Behold the death-stains on the face,
   And see what gory blood is spilt :

Conceive, what thousands in a day
   Reel at the shock which lays them low ;
That as they hang, as cold as clay,
   Ten thousand more receive the blow !

All pity's fled, when (at the fire,)
   Leg, loin, or shoulder 's on the spit,
To grace the table of the squire—
   Surrounded by things amply fit.

Where they were born, or how they live,
   On what they feed, or how they die,
Or how the little creatures grieve
   When on the butcher's block they lie

Ne'er strikes th' attention of the guest,
  Host, hostess, scull'ry-maid, nor cook ;
It's—whether it be rightly drest,
  And whether "paid," or on the book.

O ! little faithfuls,—eat and drink,
  For on to-morrow you must fall :
'Tis good thou hast no thought to think ;
  Were 't so, thy lifetime would be gall.

Trip on, lie down and go to sleep,
  Run skipfully, or stand ye still ;
Feed on, as should ye—pretty sheep,
  Until thou deem'st thou 'st had thy fill ;—

No-one will grudge thee what thou 'st ta'en,
  For in return thou 'videst us food :
Ah ! through the field and narrow lane
  Thou 'rt hurried to the field of blood.

Thy jackets, shorn, are piled in store,
  Or carted to the mart for sale ;
Thy wool, O ! meek ones (woven o'er),
  Adorns the hearth, flaunts in the gale.

In every land, on every sea,
  Where commerce traverses the globe,—
'Tis knit in garb's simplicity ;
  Knit in the monarch's choicest robe ;

Knit in the infant's swaddling clothes ;
  Knit in the mother's "jaconet ;"—*

---

* A kind of knitted jacket for the body.

In colours various as the rose,
    As various as the violet,

Promiscuous 'sturchion, and (methinks)
    Still further—the chrysanthemum,
Punctilious dahlia, hornèd pinks,
    The rose-like poppy in full bloom.

Nay, more—geraniums, beauteous things,
    The ear-drop fuchsias—every kind,
And that sweet flow'r* which gently clings
    To where contentment fills the mind†.—

Not that contentment reigns alone
    In the most humble cottages,
But that it is more rarely known
    To dwell in gorgeous palaces.

—◇◇—

A School Festival.‡

AMONG the fern, the chestnut, and the oak,—
Beside the stilly lake and silent brook,—
A host of little boys and maidens play
With pastors, masters, keeping holiday.

---

* The woodbine.   † The peasant's cot.
‡ Composed on the occasion of St. Peter's (Pimlico, London) annual
School Festival, held at Bushy Park, Hampton Court, 27th July, 1865.

Their merry whistle and their shrill-voic'd tongues,
The hip-hurrahs join'd with their youthful songs,
Make one glad concert of unusual mirth—
One happy unison of joy on earth.
They tumble, rumble, on the beauteous lawn,
As free from care as are the swift-foot fawn
That stray beneath yon summer-blooming trees,
And sniff at will the heav'nly-perfum'd breeze.
See how the little rev'lers romp and fall,
Whilst some are racing for the sky-thrown ball :
A stripling, heedless of th' obscurèd root
Of some large chestnut, trips his nimble foot,
And stumbles; but 'tis only o'er a mound,
Clad with Earth's velvet, so no harm is found.

There (laughingly) th' expectant bride,
Is sporting lovingly with him—her pride :
Then sprightly tripping to another, tries
To startle him, who (turning round) espies
Her merry-making face, and laughs consent,—
Whilst she discloses some blithe sentiment.

*   *   *   *   *   *

Look round again : there seems a sweet content
In every eye ; in every bosom seems
A heart that beats with love's enchanting beams.
List to the music of th' refection bell :
Behold the young ones,—e'en their gestures tell
What speaks it ; they come hast'ning to its ting,
And form themselves, adroitly, in a ring
Upon the trodden blade. They sit, and eat,
And quaff. Why should they not ?—It is most meet
Those Englanders should well enjoy their treat.

Hear then the thunder of the little throat
Of him, who first doth nail* the Pastor's coat,—
Of them, who follow—anxious for the prize,
Which is held out to greet their longing eyes—
As forth the Pastor runs from tree to tree,
With equal pleasure and sincerity.

*   *   *   *   *   *

Now for the elder ones : they, like the young,
Refresh'd, hie forth and mingle with the throng,
As prone to mirth, apparently as gay
As Spring's sweet blossoms in the bright noon-day :
Some tune their voices in harmonious glee,
And thus make jub'lant the festivity ;
Whilst others, wand'ring o'er the pleasant grounds,
Return to welcome those according sounds,
And bid them echo, with their meet applause,
The blitheful song in honour of the cause.

Again the ball is launch'd upon the green :
But lo !—down west, day's radiant lamp is seen
In gorgeous amplitude. The hour has come—
The junior host are marshall'd out for home.
God then is prais'd :† and, as the heav'ns grow dark,
The deer are left the guardians of the park.

---

* Make holdfast.   † The singing of a hymn.

An Autumnal Day.*

WHEN Morn,† returning, upward leaps
    Into the realms of day—
Re-gilding mountain-tops, and steeps,
    Most heav'nward in the sky,
And finding unpropitious clouds
    Spread o'er the vast expanse,—
Obscuring from Earth's mingling crowds
    His needed countenance,—
He puts his golden armour on,
    Bends his portentous bow,
And sends his arrows quiv'ring down
    Direct upon the foe ;—
So swift, so pond'rously each beam
    Falls on the murky host,
Disconsolation seizes them ;
    When, gathering to their post,
Again they furiously contend
    For the supremacy ;
But they, alas ! dejected, wend
    Their course reluctantly.

   *   *   *   *   *

Now, whilst the conflict waxed hot,
    He sought the briny foam—
Return'd afresh'd, (but they were not),
    And cheer'd the peasant's home ;

---

* This poem is intended to illustrate the Sun's fleetings on the Earth's
surface, occasioned by the passage of clouds, on a breezy day.
   † The Sun.

Or stole across an emerald lawn,
   Thus dighting Nature's face,
And play'd among the bounding fawn,—
   Those youngsters of the chase ;
Then o'er the woodland, o'er the plain,
   Or down the streamlet borne—
Through grassy vales—on to the main,
   Where sailors hail blest Morn :
Now back again to the garden spot,
   Or to the infant's cheek—
Whilst rocking in the nursling cot ;
   Thence to the orchard creek ;
Perchance o'er housetops high and low,
   Against the village spire,
Or through the fane he deigns to go
   And scans the sacred choir ;
Then saunters o'er the lonely grave,
   Where mingle rich and poor :
Now off again to the crested wave ;
   Again to the old barn-door.

  *   *   *   *   *

And now the god ordains to grace
   The city ; but 'tis vain—
A sluggish mist pervades the space,
   While clouds, dispensing rain,
Lay 'cumbent o'er the busy crowd :
   At length his portly mien—
Through some one condescending cloud—
   Re-animates the scene !

  *   *   *   *   *

Ah me ! methinks those human beings,
   Who raise that murm'ring sound,

Are like a myriad little things
    Which hither—thither bound—
Unstable as the sandy shore,
    As restless as the sea—
Receding, curling, toppling o'er,
    For all eternity.

   *   *   *   *   *

And when he once more skirts the sky—
    Down gliding in the west—
Observe the tim'rous clouds which fly,
    Carnation'd, to the east :—
O ! watch the gorgeous king of day,
    Descending, gone from view * * *
Ah ! who shall live to rise, and pray,
    As he comes round anew ?—
And that he will ; but who shall see
    The god as round he rolls ?—
It may be—Immortality
    Hath claim'd a thousand souls !

   *   *   *   *   *

Some live to see the glorious Sun
    Descend the great concave ;
But thousands, ere the day is done,
    Are silent in the grave ! ! !

Our Little Brother.*

'Tis night! 'tis night! the solemn hour is come ;
A storm-toss'd bark, "'lexandra," 's on the foam :
    Sound an alarm ere she is rift !
    To Heaven a hundred eyes uplift :
    His Answer comes as doubly swift,—
The winds abate ; calm is the crested main,
The goodly craft rides on in peace again.

Touch, touch the thread, which stretches land and sea ;
Command it bear the news, with accuracy,
    Through channels, rivers, lakes, and rills ;
    Through England's vales, o'er Scotland's hills :
    Through Ireland's uplands, creeks, and dells,—
" Ere proud Aurora flush'd the purple East,
The Danish bark was safe, and sleeps at rest."

Sound, sound the cymbal, sound the silver horn ;
Herald afar " a Prince to-day is born : "
    Tell Denmark's King, " Safe is his child,
    That the Great God in kindness smil'd ;
    A nation's heart is reconciled : "
Tell him " his Daughter is old England's pride ;
That in our love she alway may confide."

Send forth the word unto Balmoral halls,—
" That pray'rs were said within our sacred walls,

* Written on the occasion of the birth of Prince George Frederick Ernest
Albert, second son of their Royal Highnesses the Prince and Princess of
Wales, at Marlborough House, Pall Mall, 3rd June, 1865, at 1.18.

To Him above, the gracious Giver,
For her, for him, and his for ever :
All hail the little princely brother !"
On British hearts, engraven is the word—
" Our crown and country rules with one accord."

O Lord, inspire the mother's tender breast,
That she may offer up her thanks, the best ;
   And have, in Thee, the surest friend,
   To-day, and to a distant end ;
   Down on her children comfort send :
Bless, Thou, the haven which the shelter gave ;
Guard sire, and dame, and children to the grave !

The Coming of the Belgians.*

Hoist, Britons, hoist the banner high !—
   Blow the blithe horn ! blow merrily on ;
Ring out its welcome in the sky,
   And herald forth to Wimbledon
Our warrior-guests from Belgium-land :
   From Belgium land they come, they come
To share with us in Britons' land
   The banquet-board and social home.
Right welcome shall those warriors be
   To Britons' land, to Britons' land,

* Return visit of the Belgian Volunteers (to England), July, 1867.

For they have come across the sea
  To Britons' land, to Britons' land.

  Hoist, Britons, hoist the banner high ! —
    Blow the blithe horn ! blow merrily on ;
  Ring out its welcome in the sky :
    Hurrah ! hurrah ! for Wimbledon.

'Tis there our laurels now are won—
  Where bloom the gorse's golden flower,
And where the butterfly, anon,
  Doth sport amid the bramble bower ;
And where the heather dights the plain,
  Where Nature, in its forest trim,
Delights the eye, perfumes the main :
  Where every daisy is a gem ;
Where soars the cuckoo's glad ding-dong,
  And the sweet blackbird's merry air ;
Aye ! where the skylark's matin song
  Is, is of all the sweetest pray'r.

  Hoist, Britons, host the banner high ! etc.

'Tis there th' elect of Englishmen,
  And Scotland's fairest sons of might,
Bemake the upland grove and glen,
  The pinnacle of fame and fight :
'Tis there Hibernia's children hie,
  Join'd by the men of ancient Wales.
For Honor's prize each country vie ;
  Ho ! ho ! ye plains, ye hills, ye vales ;
Ho ! ho ! my kinsmen, ho ! and hail
  Our brother Belgians from afar,

Who now (responsive) westward sail,
　　To join in modern modes of war.

　　　Hoist, Britons, hoist the banner high ! etc.

To join in modern modes of war
　　They came, our brother Belgians come,
But not for conquest, nor the star
　　Which desolates the peasant's home ;
For honor, wisdom, love, and truth,—
　　These are the prizes—these their aim :
Behold those patriots, age and youth,
　　All marksmen for their country's fame.
Then welcome them to Wimbledon,
　　Ye Britons bold and bolder still ;
For there the laurels shall be won
　　By those of most abundant skill.

　　　Hoist, Britons, hoist the banner high ! etc.

'Tis there our countrymen advance
　　On the high road to royal regard,
For there shall Edward nobly glance
　　On Britain's patriotic guard.
Then on ! ye willing warriors, on !
　　Unfurl the standard, lift it high,
And let it wave o'er Wimbledon,—
　　A beacon to the Belgian eye.
Up with your tents, encamp ye round
　　"The flaming flag of liberty ;"
Send the swift ball forth to the mound ;
　　'Tis won !—whose is the victory ? * * *

　　　Hoist, Britons, hoist the banner high ! etc.

Let Record mark this year of grace,
    When forth the Belgian from the east,
With glowing heart and beaming face,
    Came o'er to share the British feast :
When Britain, lit with loyalty,
    Drew forth its chamois as of yore,
And deck'd with right baronialty
    The banquet-board with choicest store :
Whereat the best skill'd war-men came,
    From highlands, lowlands, vales, and plains ;
And where the foremost heard his name
    Proclaim'd in proud triumphant strains.

Hoist, Britons, hoist the banner high !—
    Blow the blithe horn ! blow merrily on ;
Proclaim aloud the victory !—
    Hurrah ! hurrah ! for Wimbledon !

A Song : " Willy " and Anne.

" WILL you write to me, love, when away,—
    When poor ' Willy ' 's gone over the lake !*—
If you will, I will promise to pay
    Thee for all the sweet labour you take ?"

" Yes !"—she said, with a faint yet sweet voice—
    " But be sure you fail not, in your turn,

* Signifying the sea.

To write back to the maid of your choice,—
   If 'tis me then she'll long your return."

Singing on—said he " Oh ! I'll not fail,
   If the heavens are kind to the ship,—
Safely wafting her on with the gale,—
   And we reach the French port of Dieppe."

" Ah then !—when you are there," said sweet Anne,
   " Will you send by the first coming post?"—
(With the same, a small pearl over-ran)—
   And she sigh'd—"else I'll think you are lost !"

Singing on—said he, " Can you forget
   Our last ramble beneath the bright moon,
When your ' Willy,' and you, loving sat
   On the gate-stile, and watch'd it go down ?"

" Never ! never !" she said, "for e'en now
   Thy dear arms I feel round me entwin'd,
With thy lips on my unveiled brow,
   Whilst the zephyrs were wafting behind."

A Song : The Lost Merchantman.

DIRE is the night !—fleet lightnings flash
    Across the sombre main ;
The thunders roll ; the surges lash ;
    Terrific is the rain :
The quiv'ring ship looks straight a-head,—
    She strives to face the storm,—
When lo—the mainmast's struck, and fled !—
    Now her dismantled form
Reels piteously upon the wave,—
    She mourns her broken beam ;
And the poor seaman sees his grave
    Within the turb'lent cream.

Unhappy ship !—unhappy ship !—
    Ah ! but an hour before
Light as a fairy didst thou skip ;
    And merrily on you bore
Your burden o'er the field of blue—
    Trimm'd like a lovely girl—
Until the ghastly tempest grew,
    And all hands 'gan to furl
Thy sails, to shun the dread " white squall,"—
    That most unwelcome guest,—
The most portentous foe of all
    Upon the ocean's breast.

The minute-gun booms, but in vain ;
    Her ropes shriek in the gale ;

Alas! her "midship" 's rent in twain :
    The Captain, he looks pale,
And—faltering—sighs, and drops a tear,
    But brave unto the last :
Now, conscious that his end is near,
    (The ship was sinking fast)
Appeals for all to Him on high !
    His orisons have flown ;—
" Farewell," he said to one " hard by,"
    Then with the ship went down ! ! !

London, October 2nd, 1865.

𝕱riend 𝕮harles——.*

I'm glad, Dear C., to find you're living still ;
And thank you for the usual quinine pill :
Be pleas'd t' accept—more than the sum you crave—
Two extra postage-stamps, with which pray have
One glass of Bass'——to cheer thy trusty heart :
May ten years more (if spared to thee) impart
A better spirit to thy chast'ning health :
Altho', like me—thou may'st lack worldly wealth,
Thou hast a soul symbolical of love,—
Yet never ventur'd in the Hymeneal grove !

* A few lines on the author's receipt of a box of pills from an old acquaintance (C. H.) of Ashburton.

Whate'er inquiries might be made for me
Among thine own, and my fraternity,
'Tell them I'm blithe (tho' scanty is my purse),
And that I care not one brave " cobbler's curse"
For all the riches other men enjoy ;
I do my best, my energies employ
To pay the sixpence where there's any due,—
And therefore settle my account with you.

The Fallen Leaf.

AUTUMN's here : the leaves are flitting,
Thousands o'er the fields are tripping,—
    O ! watch them as they fall :
Go, eye them as they leave the tree,
All fluttering down reluctantly
    Across the beams of Sol.

See ye the Sun—far down the west—
As he goes forth (as 'twere to rest),
    And bids one half* " Good-night ?" * * *
Well—tens of thousands go with him
Down o'er that bank with gilded brim ;
    Whilst the proud sky is dight

* One hemisphere.

With clouds, like flowers of beauteous tint
Strewn o'er the heav'nly continent
    And capering with the breeze—
Stretch'd far and wide and circling round,
And frisking through the vast profound,
    As leaves frisk from the trees.

D'ye ween the meaning of my line ?—
When Sol goes down that great incline,
    I'd have ye think, with me,
That thousands have gone o'er the hill—
Whilst he goes on revolving still—
    Unto eternity !

If right ye ween, I'd have you be—
Yea ! like that orb—as readily
    Prepared to leave the Earth.
Ye high, ye low, ye rich, ye poor,
Ye crownèd head, ambassador,—
    No matter rank or birth,—

Reflect ye : for, like as the leaf
Falls down without a sign of grief,
    Nor deigns to heave a sigh,
The monarch or the statesman must
Fall down and crumble into dust—
    As all are born to die !

Altho' we* mourn for one now gone,
And he—that grey-hair'd Palmerston,†

---

* The nation.

† The Right Honourable Henry John Temple, Viscount Palmerston.
K.G., G.C.B., &c. ,the then Premier of the British Government), died at

We will give God the praise,—
For he, beyond the age of man,*
Eleven years had over-ran
Within two equal days.

London, 18th October, 1865.

The Gout.

THAT enemy—the gout, I ween,
Of all such demons is most keen :
Some clever people seem to think
It is the treach'rousness of drink ;
But where's there one who fain would bear
Such agony for wine or beer,
Or any other kind of cheer?—
Stuff, and all nonsense : yet, no doubt,
Some drinks are feeders to the gout.

Rare Doctor Jenner, whom we praise,
Regarded not this foul disease ;
Or if he did, 'tis plain that he
Could not invent a remedy.
Oh ! would he had devised a plan
To extirpate the gout from man :

"Brockett Hall," Herts, at a quarter to eleven o'clock in the forenoon of
Wednesday, 18th October, 1865, aged eighty-one years (all but two days),
having been born on the 20th October, 1784. The above lines were written
on the occasion of his death.

* Scriptural limitation.

Much praise would then ascend to Heaven
For all the comfort he had given.
  But if man must for e'er endure
(For lack of any kingly cure)
To the world's end this evil thing,
I say—God grant unto the king,
Or queen, or statesman, be who 't may,
A life no longer than a day !—
For surely 'tis a sin to wish
The gouty monster to a fish.

*   *   *   *   *   *

Would there were men, with wit enow,
This nevious demon could subdue ;
I would, for one, bestir the stars
To introduce them to famed Mars,
To Jupiter, or Mercury,—
(Together or alternately,)—
That theirs may be felicity
For evermore.   And, farther still,
I'd have their names engraven well
Upon a diamond monument,—
An everlasting testament,—
Recording all their virtues on 't—
What they had done with liniment,
Without it or with medicines. —

*   *   *   *   *   *

(Now, if I thought 'twere treach'rous wines,
Rums, brandies, whiskies, or champagnes,
Which set this venom in man's veins,
I'd have the sea drink all the trash.   *   *   *
Give me the bottles for to smash !—

For not one dog* shall e'er remain
To give man such infernal pain.)—

*   *   *   *   *   *

And more than this†—I'd have them driven
Across the great concave of heaven,
In chariots wrought of solid gold;
Choice diamonds, rubies, gems untold,
Should be inlaid about its sides;
And flying horses (o'er their hides
'Boss'd bullion-trappings, chaste and neat)
Should from their heads down to their feet
Be clad with   *   *   *   *   ;
That gods may envy those proud beings
Who drove from man those evil things—
The gout! the gout! the gout! the gout!—
    I turn again my muse about,
And fancy yet I can't refrain
From lauding in the highest strain—
(As 'twere—with organs, great in tone,
Reverb'rating from zone to zone,
And angels rivalling to intone
Their universal notes of joy;
Whilst all the hosts of heaven deploy
In armour wrought by gods of grace,
And shining through th' ethereal space
With so much splendour that 'tis meet
One closed his eyes against the treat)—
These men who could the cure complete.

*   *   *   *   *   *

---

* Bottle.
† The introduction to Mars, Jupiter, Mercury, &c.

Old Doctor Samuel* said (I'm told) —
A pyramid of solid gold,
As high as heav'n—or higher still—
For him who could the villain kill,
Ought to be built upon a hill.

    Aye ! thousands would improve the pen,
In ecstasies, to praise the man,
Or rhetorise in words of bliss —
" To him perpetual happiness
Should be awarded from on high,
For ridding that dire enemy."   *   *   *

    Oh ! what a song of joy I'd write
If I could hear it said to-night·—
" The plaguy rogue was kill'd outright."

    Alas ! (I am most loath to state)
I fear not one, so fortunate,
Will ever be the poor man's friend
To bring this d——l to an end.

* Doctor Samuel Johnson.

The Fox's Lair.

BLEAK is that spot, prone to the west,
　When winter lays it bare,
And when among those rocks the blast
　Moans harshly on the ear.

But there, though bleak, though rough, though
　　wild,
　Old Reynard makes his bed,
And shelter'd by those rocks, beguil'd,
　Serenely rests his head.

Therein he lurks the livelong day,
　There sleeps the wily thief;
He, like a robber, plans for prey,
　But comes at last to grief.

Around and 'bout those mossy stones,
　Wherein the felon prowls,
Lay strewn a thousand tiny bones—
　The sunder'd frames of fowls,

Of lambs, and other innocents,
　Bred to have 'dorn'd the plate :
Those sundry farm-yard 'habitants
　Met a most wretched fate !

The sunbeams gild not Reynard's brow,
　He shuns it with dismay ;

He feeds not with the old milch-cow
    In open fields of day.

The last streaks of the sunken Joy
    Are signals to advance ;
Then the foul cave he leaves so coy,
    And like a rogue doth glance

Below, above ; his eyes roll round,
    He sniffs the breath of night :
All's silent now,—no yelping sound
    Prevents his hasty flight.

Out, and upon his deathly track,
    The coppice combs his hair ;
Instinctively he weens his back
    Will have a prize to bear.

Behold him on the farm-yard fence,
    Surveying the peaceful fold :
See how the tartar sneaks from thence—
    Ah ! see—his jaws have hold ! * * *

His little lambkin victim dies :
    Then, with accustom'd skill,
He hurls it on his back, and flies
    Home to the stony-hill.

There in his haunt (rocks and dank earth),
    The daring burglar spills
His victim's blood, with brigand's mirth,
    And sends it forth in rills * * *

Next morn, as usual, all the flock
   Is counted o'er, and o'er,—
Suspicion is arous'd—the stock
   Is minus one ! (not more)—

The farmer hurriedly looks 'round,
   Unwilling to believe
His little lamb's not to be found,
   Then he begins to grieve :

So 'round and 'round the yard he paced,
   Scann'd every thought-of nook ;
At length upon the fence he traced
   The course the rebel took.

Beyond the fence a narrow pass
   Through thick-grown furze led on
To where there was a patch of grass,
   A spot both dank and lone ;

Here turn'd the fiend through dwarfish oak,
   Which stretch'd up half a mile,
Then nimbly cross'd a limpid brook,
   And gain'd the granite pile.

Long ere the farmer reach'd this den
   The wolfish feast was past :
He mourn'd his lost one, but 'twas vain,
   And said—" This is thy last."

Six rough-hair'd terriers, fresh from sleep,
   All eager for the fray,

Compell'd the laughing fiend to weep
Before it was noon-day.

The clacking of each battle dog
Surprised the sharp-nosed thief;
Who doubtless stood shrunk like a slug,
Yet desperate in his grief.

Now raged the conflict doubly fierce:
Uncertain which had won,
The farmer listen'd: shrieks then pierce
His ear: he listen'd on—

Alas! he miss'd his favourite's voice—
His darling's tongue was hush'd;
From him—the warrior-dog of choice—
Life's stream had freely gush'd,

Though his was not the only wound:
A pause: now all is mute:—
Then came five grisly dogs to ground;
They limp—the pain 's so 'cute.

Spill'd blood bespatter'd each rough skin,
Which spoke the dreadful strife
That murderously had raged within,
With sacrifice of life.

Yes! out they came, and bore along
The corpse of their slain mate:—
The farmer's heart was sorely wrung
To see his favourite's fate!

The Petrified Nest.[*]

THIS bulfinch' nest, which you behold,
For thirty pence to me was sold :—
Bound round with tape, and fix'd in place,
Was petrified in twelve months' space ;
Then taken down, brought to the inn,
Where " Mother Shipton's" sign is seen —
(Herself, the dear old lady's drawn
In antique mantle, hood, and gown,)—
On which is writ, as trav'lers see,
The following lines of poetry—
" Near to this petrifying well,
I first drew breath. as records tell."

  *   *   *   *   *   *

O Knaresboro', Knaresboro' ! charms are thine ;
Thee,[†] thousand beauties do combine :
Oh ! would that thou wert my abode,—
Thou glorious spot inwrought by God !
With Him no workman can compare ;
His skilful works are everywhere :
And He alone did carve the world,
Round which the mighty ocean curl'd.
  Incumbent rocks, as they were hurl'd,

---

* These lines were composed to accompany the nest, which the author
purchased at the little museum of petrified curiosities in " Mother Shipton's" Inn, situated about a quarter of a mile from the Dropping Wells at
Knaresborough, and which he presented to his much respected friend and
benefactor, J. Cutcliffe, Esq., then residing at Newcastle-under-Lyme,
Staffordshire, August, 1865.
 † Use the article " a."

H

And mountains, tow'ring to the skies,
And verdant valleys, greet our eyes.
  Here, ancient castles (once so grand)
Show marks of Time's defacing hand ;
Some, shatter'd by war's hissing shot,
Leave only stones to tell the spot ;
Whilst others, towers still abide
To mourn, alas ! their former pride :
And thine, O Knaresboro', shares the fall—
Now little but a crumbling wall.

The Kingly Oak* of Bagot's Park.†

THE fearless monarch—old, yet hale,
    More proud than in his youth—
Laughs and enjoys the passing gale,
    Is happy ; and—forsooth--

He's like a king (who chance be good)
    Surrounded by his court,
Or like a lord of merry mood,
    Obtains a meet report.

He loves the fair one's gentle touch,
    The squeeze of hardier hands ;

---

* Supposed to be more than two centuries old.   † In Staffordshire.

And with a bow—no elms can match—
    Conveys " he understands."

Two hundred winters now have fled
    Since forth the seedling came ;
A hundred more may crown his head,
    Ere his is but a name.

Soft zephyrs shall caress his crown,
    And curl around his form ;
Horus, of old, shall oft go down ;
    While many a dreadful storm

Shall drench the monarch to the skin,
    And ravage Bagot's Park,
Ere his stout heart shall yield within
    Its noble coat of bark.

Though grand his mien, he never boasts,
    Nor e'er usurps the green ;
But loves to see the minor hosts
    Salute his distant queen.*

Many a tourist scans this oak :†
    Some, measuring round his base,‡
Exclaim, " 'Tis worth a march to look
    Upon his fine old face !"

Now when he's angry (true 'tis not
    That often he doth frown),

---

* Another very large oak, called the "Queen."
† The King.
‡ About twenty-four feet round, as measured by the author (of the poem
and his friend, Mr. E. Emery, of Abbots Bromley.

And when the winds, concerting, plot
   To hurl him from his throne,

'Tis then he asserts his majesty.
   And lifts his powerful voice ;
But when the storm hath passèd by.
   You will again rejoice

To see him as he deigns to laugh
   And gently bend his head,
Inviting you to come, and quaff
   Upon the grassy bed,—

(On which, and 'round about, regale
   The antler'd buck, and deer,
And goats, and feather'd tribes,) t' inhale
   The perfumes of the year.

Profoundly silent,* acres lay
   Invig'rated by Time ;
Whilst shelt'ring woodlands make them gay,
   And deck the favour'd clime.

O ! may'st thou† live to teach the young
   The secret of that gift,
Through which thou'st grown so great, so
      strong,
   Before thy trunk is rift ;

---

* Land, in its forest-like condition.
† The " Kingly Oak '

That each may wear upon his brow,
    Like thine—an honest mark,
And so retain, as thou dost now,
    The pride of " Bagot's Park."*

SONG.

Up, up, my Brave Comrades ! †

(An Exhortation to the Volunteers.)

Up, up, my brave comrades ! with courage abounding,
Don your pouches and rifles—the bugle is sounding ;
As our fathers of old quickly 'rose for the fray—
Up, up, and reply to its chivalrous lay :
And although its shrill blast bears no tidings of war,
Nor the boom of the gun on the ocean afar
Tells of death and destruction, yet of you we have
    need
For the weal of our Country, our Throne, and our
    Creed.
        Up, up, my brave comrades ! with courage
            abounding,
        Don your pouches and rifles—the bugle is
            sounding ;

---

* This poem was composed during the author's visit to his friend, J. C——,
Newcastle-under-Lyme, Sept., 1865.
† Composed on the occasion of the first Volunteer Review at Dover, on
Easter Monday, 22nd April, 1867.

As our fathers of old quickly 'rose for the fray—
Up, up, and reply to its chivalrous lay.

Go forth, my brave comrades! the bugle hath sounded;
As of old let the foemen, who dare, be confounded;
But, thank God, there's no foe—there's no enemy near
To encounter the arm of our brave Volunteer:
Yet of you we have need, for our Throne and our
    hearth
Will be safe whilst protected by men of such worth :—
Therefore comrades go forth with a smile and a cheer,
For our country hath hope in the brave Volunteer.
      Up, up, my brave comrades! with courage
        abounding, &c.

March on, my brave comrades! the bugle's still
    sounding;
On your path the hurrahs of a nation's resounding;
And on yon foremost plain where the host shall
    deploy,
There shall echo the anthem of love and of joy :
There the contest of peace shall envelop the wold,
While the blue waves are dancing in spangles of gold;
While the clouds from your rifles obscure the blithe
    sky,
We'll reflect and thank God there's no foe to defy!—
      Up, up, my brave comrades! with courage
        abounding, &c.

𝔄 𝔏𝔢𝔱𝔱𝔢𝔯 𝔱𝔬 𝔥𝔦𝔰 𝔏𝔬𝔯𝔡𝔰𝔥𝔦𝔭.

76, Upper Ebury Street, Pimlico, S.W.,
6th May, 1865.

MY LORD,

I've scann'd your answer to my meek request,
Which prompts the feeling in my studious breast—
A silent hoping—that, some future day,
My pen may gain thy Lordship's solacy.

  ※   ※   ※   ※   ※

Being train'd to disappointment, trust me, lord,
I lie not down ; but steadfast to my word,
Shall persevere with all my heart and soul ;
Shall still dip pens into the inken-bowl ;
Shall strive to write my F (two) o o (and) t,
And trust they'll grace a book of poetry,—
If not of merit such as Wits admire,
I must expect their silence, or satire :
Ah ! should it be the latter, I obtain,
'Twill be encouragement to try again.
 O, had I but a tithe of Alfred's * spark,
I'd launch again my little hopeful bark,
Into the ocean of my soul's delight !
Would prose all day, and sometimes half the night ;
Would scribble out blank verse, or couplets, free ;
Would 'queath its pages to futurity.
And when my sand-glass had run out its last,—
My eyes for ever had been closed and fast,—

---

* Tennyson, poet laureat.

Perchance some kindred creature would have fix'd
On some plain stone, the lines herewith annex'd :—
" Oh ! grant, here—reader, but one moment's pause—
    Behold—this man did ransack o'er his brain ;
And found a word or two to help the cause,
    So strove to rhythm them in humble strain."

    *   *   *   *   *

But ere, my lord, I stop my feeble muse,
I ask of thee, and feel thou'lt not refuse,
To send me back those manuscripts of mine—
That I may write them in corrected line :
And when my scroll * is publish'd, I shall crave
Your Lordship's care of one.   (Now, to be grave)—
Pray give allowance for my ignorance—
If I am pert ; if I, through lack of sense,
Have trespass'd on your Lordship's valued time—
Some specimens of my attempted rhyme.
'Tis not my wish to cornet forth my name,
Nor can I e'er expect to gather fame,
But only hope, my lord, you kindly will
Assist me up the literary hill.

I am,

My Lord,

Your Lordship's most obedient Servant.

EDWARD E. FOOT.

To the Right Honorable
    Viscount Palmerston, K.G , &c.,
        Cambridge House, Piccadilly, W.C.

* Book.

𝔐𝔶 𝔡𝔢𝔞𝔯 𝔣𝔯𝔦𝔢𝔫𝔡 𝔍𝔬𝔥𝔫.*

PRAY, let my pen interpret now
   The silent throbbings of my heart,—
Believe me when I make this vow—
   My gratitude can ne'er depart.

Thou hast rebuked me, I must own,
   With smart precision, and 'tis just ;
But still there's with it meetly flown
   The rod of love, which ne'er can rust.

Oh ! think not this, " that I can be
   A creature without gratitude : "
On foreign lands ; the briny sea ;
   In north and southern latitude,

I've ponder'd 'neath the starry height—
   Thank'd thee, dear John, my dearest friend ;
Dwelt o'er past pleasures with delight,
   And shall till Death defines my end.

Then, let no angry thoughts possess
   Your mind, or mine ; my mind, nor your's ;
I seek to offer you redress ;
   And when thine eye upon it soars,

* Composed on the occasion of receiving a letter from his great friend,
J. Cutcliffe, Esq., complaining of the Author's negligence in correspondence,
and which "few lines" form'd part of his letter, in reply. 1865.

You, too, I'm sure, will say (with me,)
   " Come what there may—our love's the same."
So now, dear friend, pray let there be
   No future enmity, or blame.

Christmas Eve. (1864.*)

FILL the punch-bowl to the brim,
   Merry be—'tis Christmas-time,
In it let sliced lemons swim,
   'Til the midnight bell doth chime.

Eye the holly, fresh and green,
   Intertwined with mistletoe ;
Cast the ashen faggot† in,
   Fan it till it crack and glow.

Pass the rosy goblet round ;
   Bathe thy lips in liquors choice ;
Pour thy pleasure out in sound ;
   Make an effort with thy voice :

---

* Christmas Day, in this year, happened to be on Sunday.
   † In Devonshire farmhouses, it is a very customary practice, on Christmas
Eve, to put a number of wooden binders around an ashen or oaken faggot,
and according to the quantity of them the binders', so is the quantity of
cider regulated for the evening's entertainment.

Thus enhance the jubilee—
    Let fair damsels lead the songs,
Follow them, in harmony ;
    For with music love belongs.

Haste ye, and repeat the glee,
    Solo-song, or madrigal :—
Quoth the host—" It pleases me,
    Bravo !—thou hast sung it well."

Hark ! the church-clock, striking twelve,
    Tingles through the merry hall ;
Put the tankard on the shelf—
    Rich or poor,—and stop the ball.*

Now, with solemn gratitude,
    Thank Him, who provides us cheer ;
And with equal promptitude
    Reverence the fast fleeting year.

Spend the Sabbath, ('tis the last
    That will count in 'sixty-four,)—
With a right becoming fast,
    'Til the Monday sun shall soar.

Then with seemly merriment,
    'Neath the mistletoe be gay ;
And with chasty sentiment
    Join the choral roundelay.

* The dance.

Dance together, young and old,
　To the sound of violin :
Who will venture—who so bold—
　To assert it is a sin ?—

Thus, for youths, in measured pace,
　To trip o'er the planken floor ;
Parents, with their wonted grace,
　Skipping as in days of yore ?

No ! this never can be sin,—
　So dance on— enjoy the hour ;
And when done—go, think of Him,
　Who, alone, can blessings show'r.

THE

DEATH, BURIAL, AND DESTRUCTION

OF

𝕭𝖆𝖈𝖈𝖍𝖚𝖘 ;

OR,

THE FRUITS OF LASCIVIOUSNESS.

AN ALLEGORICAL POEM,

IN

TWO CANTOS.

BY

E. E. FOOT.

PROLOGUE.—It may be considered presumptuous of the Author that he should have dared to venture in the paths of Allegory; but since he has been guilty of doing so, he must bear whatever chastisement may be inflicted upon him. The Poem is intended, in the first instance, to illustrate in a figurative manner the frailty of the human mind—or rather, the natural propensity of the human heart—in the pursuit of pleasure; which, if not mercifully prevented by the interposition of Divine Providence, tends to create an insatiate desire for new and un-attainable delights; fosters an intemperate habit; promotes an incessant craving after carnal joys; and which inevitably involves a person in the whirlpool of vice, and ultimately leads to the destruction of the Soul. In the second instance, to depict (according to the Author's humble ideas) the manner of mystic glorification—instituted by the Sovereign of the Outer World—continually going on in the dominions of his Satanic Majesty; but which, to the unredeemed souls of departed creatures, is the sad state of everlasting torment, consequent to perdition. And thirdly, the Author hopes this representation * of the unblissful regions may have the effect of retarding, at least—in some degree, the appetite for the pleasures, or he would say: vanities of this life; and of eventually averting the evil and direful calamity, by—"Turning the hearts of the disobedient unto the wisdom of the just."

* For it scarcely can be believed that there is such a place in reality—viz., of a tangible nature; but if so, in what direction of the boundless Pro-found can it be? and where are we to look for it?

The Death, Burial, and Destruction of Bacchus.

CANTO THE FIRST.

SEE, sweetly cluster'd, that gigantic vine,*
Whose globes ambrosial swell with virgin wine? * * *
There you behold, enthroned in majesty—
With all the honors due to royalty
And state—the sovereign source of harmony !
    *   *   *   *   *

A thousand branches stretch out far and wide,
And every branch adds to her queenly pride :
Yet she hath many sorrows to endure ;
For, as the season comes from year to year,
The pruner's blade (like as the surgeon's knife)
Makes deep incisions to prolong her life.
Oh ! how she mourns when one by one are fled
Those purple beauties which she bore and bred,
And nurtur'd in the glory of her age—
The admiration of her country's sage :
Contrast her fan-like leaves with her choice fruit ;
Trace her frail topmost tendril to its root,
When Horus† upon high sends down his beams,
And sheds his golden bounty forth in streams,

---

* The venerable grape-vine at Hampton Court Palace, near London.
† A title of the Sun.

Beneath and round about her dwelling-place ;
And say--hast thou e'er seen such ample grace,
One lovelier, or goodlier in mien,
Than she, the great terrestrial vineyard Queen ?
　Turn now and view those Oriental climes—
The golden fountain of the rarest wines,
To-day, resembling the to-day of yore,
Yielding their complements of luscious store ;
Observe the varied hues, and fragrancy,
When fiery Leo's* in th' ascendancy.
　'Twas there that Bacchus† strove t' obtain a glimpse
Whilst the imperial company of nymphs,
Assembled at the high command of Jove,
Were interchanging sentiments of love !—
And where Apollo,‡ with unusual strains
Inspired his instrument, and thus obtains
The fairest goddess of the mystic throng ;
Who, dumb with the enchantment of his song,
Makes loving gestures that she heeds his suit ;
He, in return, becomes as equally mute :
But his fair countenance pourtray'd his heart :
Then full of joy they wing'd their golden cart,
And vanish'd in th' ethereal realms of bliss.
　Now, when the other nymphs Apollo miss,
They veil'd their faces with their flowing hair,
And smote their bosoms, sighing in despair,—
Weeping lamentingly,—for each in vain
Had sought the great musician's hand to gain :

* The zodiacal sign for July.
† The god of wine and sensuality.
‡ Represented in this poem as the great Mythological Musician ; who fell violently in love with the nymph Daphne, famed for her modesty.

Not as before—bewitchingly in gait—
But lovelorn now, and openly await
Each for a god or whomsoever may
Possess the courage to come there to play.
   Bacchus, not oftentimes as then so shrewd,
Saw his advantage, and his aim pursued :
He, great in stature, bearded to the waist,
True to his character (refresh'd with rest),
Avail'd himself of Leo's brightest hour,
And deign'd to love. Nought could withstand his power.
Like a fat ox, his loins were fair to view,—
The pith of happiness,—he never knew
What sorrow was. Ashamed, the nymphs now hide,
And in their hiding-place they scan his side
But not a sound escapes their lovely lips :—
The while, he taps a thousand globes and sips
Until he staggers, and falls prone to ground :
Then haste the nymphs, the god they circle round !
   'Tis vain attempting to describe the joy
Each goddess felt as they tripp'd round so coy :—
One, stray'ng beyond the bound'ry they had plann'd,
Most inadvertently trod on his hand ;
Which 'lectrified the god ! then he updrew,
Rais'd both his arms, and, like a trumpet, blew
A sound across the purple-cluster'd plain.
Altho' he lack'd Apollo's dulcet strain,
The nymphs admired him for his manly look,
For when he moved the very vineprops shook ;
Yea—when he spake, the clouds obey'd his voice,
And stood divided that he might rejoice
Beneath the oriental mid-day sky,
With Sol direct on his revolving eye.

His golden goblet, he with outstretch'd arms
(Which, with the god, possess'd peculiar charms),
Held forth towards the sun !—when there advanced
A hundred nymphs, on whom, like fire he glanced :
Bold as a warrior he induced them all
To come and drink from out his flowing bowl !
The nymphs, unable to resist, attend
Obediently to Bacchus's command :
The god surveys them as they raise the cup,
And, as they drink in turn, he fills it up ;—
When all have drunk their loving draught, the god
Lifts high the goblet, and vouchsafes a nod,
And bids the mistress of the fairy throng
Arrange the company to join in song ;
She, in obedience to the god's command,
Waved her white beam, and thus commenc'd the
    band :—
The high sopranos rock the fragrant breeze,
And lift their voices up by slow degrees
Until they reach the pinnacle of sound ;
The first great stanza done, then, most profound,
The sweet contraltos follow in their course—
Ascending and descending with much force
And regulated emphasis ; and then,
Uniting, send into the sunnied main
One burst of harmony ! the god then leapt,
And—overwhelm'd with ecstasy—he wept.

     *   *   *   *   *

O, what a sight it must have been to see
Great Bacchus on his throne of ivory,
Reviewing those fair daughters of the moon,
When they struck off their soul-enraptured tune !

For there he sat, crown'd with the purple vine,
And by his side his goblet of red wine :
At every strain which lifted up his soul
The monarch smil'd, and bow'd, inclined the bowl :
Again, again, he smote his sunburnt breast,
And sent Orion * to hunt down a beast,—
To Comus † also to prepare a feast,—
That he might entertain the goddesses,
And make them creatures of much happiness.

  So Bacchus, rev'ling thus in his desires,
With flooded brain to heav'n at once aspires.
His saffron body sweated down in rills.
At length, o'erpower'd, he frenzically calls
To Jupiter,‡ " O Brother, come to me,
Bring down five thousand gods to help the glee !
O mighty and most gentle Venus,§ give,
Give gen'rously thy aid that I may live !—
Bring with thee all thy own elect of stars,
Invite our friends —the brave and glorious Mars,
And lordly Herschel,‖ junior of the skies ;
And Mercury,¶ with those sharp propitious eyes :
Tell Saturn,** also, that I would he 'd come
To share with me the comforts of my home :
Earth, goodly creature, is already here
With bountiful provision of good cheer :

* A mighty hunter.
† The god of festivals.
‡ The sovereign lord of the Mythological Heaven.
§ The goddess of Beauty daughter of Jupiter .
‖ A planet known as the " Georgium Sidus :"—no mythological title.
¶ The god of Eloquence, &c.
** The most ancient of all the Heathen Deities ; the emblem of Time.

I fain would Sol invite, but fear my fate,
Lest the great god should think himself too great :
O! what a blaze of glory there would be
If he would condescend to join the glee
But for an hour, or even but a half:
O! would not Bacchus bid the guests to quaff,
Each with a goblet bumper'd up to brim?
And would not Bacchus even worship him?

      *   *   *   *   *

"Tis best, perhaps, that Sol should not come down,
For fear my darling Venus might be stol'n :
So bid my chosen-ones bring all their moons!"--
He pauses, mutters, bows his head, and swoons ;
Falls (but unhurt) with force upon the ground,
Which vibrates earth and air for miles around.

      *   *   *   *   *

Thus, senseless, for three hours low laid the god,
And by his side his golden-headed rod.
Then, gather'd 'round him, all the fairy hosts--
Pale and affrighted, like so many ghosts--
Perform a solemn requiem for his soul.
    Still stood the sun, and dark ; but in the bowl,*
The rosy liquid flamed a cubit high,
To mourn poor Bacchus' death : those standing by
Withdrew in sorrow ; one by one they fled,--
For all conceiv'd their benefactor dead !
Then rose a cloudling, circular in shape,
Of matchless beauty, tinted like the grape ;

---

* Of Bacchus.
    NOTE.--The Author has taken the liberty to use the celestial deities in
this poem in the category of planets, and to give to each of them the imaginary character of a person.

Its outer edge, fring'd round with silvery foil,
Bent gently downwards, archlike, to the soil;
So that an hemisphere of cloud conceal'd
The god's huge body from the open field.

To Bacchus' prayers * the heavenly orbs attend,
And with precision to the earth descend:
They search the vineyard o'er from end to end;
'Round and about they trip, with angels' speed;
Alas, they falter! then they (all agreed)
Cry unto Bacchus—" Bacchus! Bacchus! where—
Where art thou gone? Behold thy guests are here,—
All clothed in kingly garments of the best
We've come, as bidden, down to join the feast;
Each with a garland delicately bloomed,
And every one his instrument well tuned:
Our cloud-wrought chariots in the heavens await
To take us back, each to his own retreat,
And thou not here! Oh, cruel god, why this?
Thou'st robbed us of anticipated bliss!—
We heard your loud petition, and came down;
But what is here? and where, where art thou gone?
Fie on thee, god! Thou'rt treacherous indeed;
For we have come to thee with utmost speed,
Aroused, in joy, to expectation's height,
And hoped for day; but lo, 'tis all as night!"

Then they confer, and hence resolved to fly
Back to their mansions in the azure sky.

    *   *   *   *   *

The clouds dispers'd, and Bacchus starts afresh,
Drinks deep the purple, which inflames his flesh;

---

* See the two preceding pages.

Sends his rude orisons again on high ;
But they heed not his pray'rs : then, with a sigh,
And almost mad, he strikes his breast, and saith :
"Ye gods, be damn'd."   And now, all in a breath,
He uttereth a prayer to him above,
Beseeching, plaintively, the mighty Jove :
"Oh, well-beloved Jove ! I pray thee, hear
My tale of sorrow, which to thee I bear.
O Jove, acquainted with my nature best,
Thou know'st, alone, the cravings of my breast ;
Fann'd by the nymphs' most inspirating strain,
I sought the bowl, and fired my foolish brain :
I cried aloud to thee, as Jupiter,
But lacked, I ween, a right interpreter :
To Venus and to Mars I rais'd my voice,
For they were three respectively my choice ;
To Georgian-Herschel, and to Mercury ;
To Saturn, but 'twas vain.   'Twas vanity,
I'll own ; yet was it not, O Jove, most cruel—
Now I am old—to treat me as a fool ?"
So he continued venting loud his pray'r :
Deserted and distracted to despair,
He tried to lift the goblet, but he fail'd ;
His strength had fled ; he found himself assail'd
And at the gate of hell !—still struggling hard,
He ope'd his mouth, but uttered not a word :
He mock'd the gods with his fast fleeting breath ;
Gave up the ghost : thus met eternal death !

  *   *   *   *   *

Three days, or more, the god lay prostrate, bare,
With naught of covering save his ruffled hair,
(And not a creature chancèd to come near,)

Stretched to his full across his bed of leaves ;
His hands were clench'd, as firm as iron greaves ;
And there he laid ; when Daphne,* passing by,
Caught the reflection of his glaring eye
(For Bacchus died not, as most mortal men,
With eyes fast shut, but open to the sun),
And, like a good Samaritan, went o'er :
Rememb'ring well the visage which he bore,
She exclaim'd aloud to her great lord† of heaven—
(As she, poor nymph, was most severely smitten)—
Crying, " Bassareus‡ lies breathless on the field !
No wounds to show he has been gored or steel'd ;
And now, aghast, his eyes still move around,
His lips are quivering, and I hear a sound
Like that of Rhadamanthus (Judge of hell),
But what his converse is I cannot tell."

    Her lord came down, most sorrowful in look,
Conn'd the dead body, and again betook
His brazen chariot in all haste, and rode
Down to the regions of the infernal god :
There was rejoicing to a great extent :—
A thousand fires lit up the firmament ;
A myriad spirits danced around the flames,
Each calling Bacchus by a thousand names,
And each, like Argus, had a hundred eyes,
Which direfully glared across the den of lies ;
Their heads were horn'd, and each horn bore a
      lamp,
Mark'd with the great immortal Pluto's stamp ;

---

* The beloved nymph of Apollo.   † Apollo.
‡ One of the names of Bacchus.

(Pluto * himself, being ninety leagues away,
Was unacquainted with this revelry—
Till Vulcan † forged a bolt with wings, and sent
It in a whirlwind unto Pluto's tent ;
Therein it stood and wrote upon the wall
The brief particulars of the carnival !
This mighty god,‡ astounded to the heart,
Made hasty preparations to depart ;
Sent forth his voice, then 'roused his gloomy host,
And travell'd 'round by the south-western coast.)
And each one held two red-hot iron beams ;
Their breath ascended in sulphurous streams :
They foamed and snorted, like hard-ridden horse,
And fled across the grim and deathy course
With comets' speed ; then stamp'd with awful force
Their ponderous forms upon th' upheaving ground,
Which sent afar a hideous crackling sound :
The foam ran down their breasts like molten
        flame,—
Too dreadful to describe by any name ;
Their mouths, when open, were like rocky caves—
Down their vast throats the Styx § rush'd in great
        waves,
And when they spat, a stench obnoxious 'rose—
Offensive to the most inured nose.
Around their waists were slung huge buffalo horns
(And farther down hung girdles of black thorns),
With which they went three times a day for drink,
And stood around that dread Avernus' brink,‖

* The Lord and Governor of Hell.   † The god of subterraneous fire.
        ‡ Pluto.   § A river of hell.
        Avernus, a lake on the borders of hell.

Without attempt from the foul task to shrink ;
Then, at a word, into the lake they went,
Whose waters were of dreadful temperament :
They plunged therein as horses gored to death,
And sent forth pois'nous vapours with their breath.
Three times a day the ghastly livid lake
Turn'd into blood, with which their thirst they 'd
    slake:
When brass-hair'd Vulcan struck his mighty gong,
Erect they stood, and join'd in woful song ;
Another beat, they stretch'd their glaring eyes,
And sent a shriek into the red-wrought skies ; *
(Conceive a thousand organs thundering forth —
From every point the compass to the north—
The tone of every pipe encompassèd
Within their frames, then only 't can be said
What was the shout those spirits sent abroad
At the command of this volcanic lord !)
Once more he beat, they rais'd a dismal moan,—
Sustain'd their voices till a day was gone :
For whilst great Vulcan held his beam on high,
They durst not breathe, nor even wink an eye.
   (Oh ! what a shocking, melancholy fate,
To be the vassals of such low estate :
Dogs upon earth are angels in a heaven,
Compared to those poor wretches who are driven
From south to north, from east to west, with wings
Like flaming firebrands, and whose mouths have stings
As deadly in their touch as adders are :
Their peace is worse than earth's most direful war !)

---

    * The fiery elements.

The wretches would have slept, but lo ! a glare
Of yellow lurid light shot through the air ;
And with it came a blast of mingled sounds,
Like as the yellings of as many hounds :
This shook the spirits' nerves ; they trembled, for
They saw and knew the cloud advancing bore
Great Pluto back to his imperial throne.
In but a twinkling of an eye were flown
A swarm of wingèd fiends with gold engraven plates,
To summon forth th' infernal potentates
To meet their lord and emperor of hell.
Then they return'd, their messages to tell.

  * * * * *

Forth came the mighty host, great in their speed
(Their fiery horses panting for the deed) :
And all sent on swift-wingèd, prong-like darts,
Which bore the numbers of their brazen carts :
('T would take a day to count the numbers o'er :)
At length they advance with a continuous roar,
Dividing as they sped the sulph'ral air,
Midst fetid vapours like the fumes of war.

 Now as they approach with a most deaf'ning noise—
Sixteen abreast arranged, to counterpoise
The basement of the cloud on which they rode—
The mighty host beheld, beheld their god !

  * * * * *

Meanwhile—the mighty Vulcan (at his works),
And all his host were welding monster dirks
Of brass and steel ; and in each point, an eye
Was fixèd to conduct it through the sky,
Where it was plann'd that at a given word
Each instrument of death should fly abroad

At equal distances, directed straight
To meet the foe who dare oppose the fête.
   In warlike attitude th' inferior fiends
Stood all abreast, and facing the west winds,
(Each held a dirk four cubits in the air,
And on their breast were brazen shields of war,)—
Full fifteen rows, each row a yard advanc'd :
And in the rear ten thousand horses pranc'd,
All cap'rison'd with choicest workmanship :
Each rider held a silver-threaded whip,
Of ponderous weight, which rested on his hip
On his right side ; whilst on the left were hung
A massive sabre and a silver gong.
Behind them were arranged each curricle,
To form a background to the spectacle :
According to their numbers in rotation,
And to the high or low degree of station
Of those great potentates, so did they stand—
Prim in their aspect and exceeding' grand.
The chariots' sides, inlaid with burnish'd gold,
Reflected all surrounding them two-fold ;
On every roof there 'rose a tow'ring rod,
Which bore the banner of each minor god ;
The charioteers wore helmets, wrought of brass ;
And all their faces shone like silver'd glass.
   From north to south three leagues of ground were
     dark,
Through this great cloud incumbent o'er the park ;
And not a voice was heard, not e'en a breath,
So strict was the command. (A second death
Was the sad fate for those who disobey'd
Th' injunctions and the laws therein decreed.)

All, conscious that their lord was on his way
Back to his seat of fame and royalty,
Now look'd direct towards the bloodshot heav'n,
Through which the god of misery was driv'n ;
The lurid light increased its sickly tint,
And shed its glare about the continent :
Near to the zenith of the mystic main
Appear'd the shadow of th' advancing train,—
Small as a hand, but rapid in its growth,—
As on they came upon the yellow path :
Great as a mountain the dire shade had grown,
When suddenly a dreadful blast was blown
By fifty heralds in the foremost cloud ;
They blew again, but fifty times more loud,
So that the atmosphere of hell did quake,
And caus'd a hissing like a python snake.
Then came the thunder of the chariot wheels,
Like cannons roaring on a thousand hills.
A thousand chariots did the train compose :
And then the tramping of the horse arose,
Fell on the ears with dire and dreadful woe
Of those who listen'd with dismay : when lo !
The   heavens   open'd!   *   *   *   Vulcan struck his
        gong,
And all the multitude burst forth in song :
Which song appall'd th' ambassador of earth,*—
The great musician, minstrel, bard of mirth,—
Who now was there with his attendant gods
Array'd in splendour, holding silver rods,

---

* Apollo—who having as it were come down from earth to intercede with
Pluto in behalf of Bacchus) is, in this instance, to be considered as one of the
earth.

To greet the Emperor, as the monarch came
Down from the clouds in crimson-colour'd flame.

   *   *   *   *   *

Apollo, garmented in robes of gold,—
His stature like a giant to behold,—
With voice unmatch'd in compass and in tone.
Pour'd forth his song, which vibrated the zone :
Its text was this—" Hail, Pluto, mighty king ; "
Then all Apollo's minstrels 'round him sing
" Hail, Pluto, mighty King !" re-echoing
The song of triumph to the utmost bounds
Of the dread region, in concordant sounds.
   The multitude manœuvred, gather'd in,
And form'd an ambient circle ; where, within,
His Majesty appointed his descent.
The vassals, marshall'd, to the rearward went,
So that the inner ring contain'd the great,—
Such as th' renownèd Minos, magistrate,
Androgeüs, his son ; then, great in name,
Stood Rhadamanthus, 'nother judge of fame ;
Æacus, Acheron ; and poor Protheus, who,
Vex'd with his form, into great Etna flew ;
And by his side Prometheus, martyr'd god,
Who form'd and fired with life a moulded clod :
There, terrible in mien, stood Mulciber,*—
He, on his breast, a group of medals bore—
Marks of distinction for those mighty things
Which he had wrought through ages past for kings ;
Then his son Cacus, junior god of fire ;
And next, perfidious Sisyphus, the liar ;

          * A title of Vulcan.

Then Erebus, son of the Invisible ; *
And grim old Charon, ferryman of hell.
    At equal distances those magnates stood
About this circle of great magnitude
Much in themselves, but all subordinate
To Pluto ; who, now in great pomp and state,
Was in their midst : there He (awaiting him
The harbinger of joy—Earth's seraphim)
With pow'rful speech and accent, call'd aloud—
" Come hither, O Apollo !"   Forth went the
        god,
When there uprose a nevious curling cloud,
Great in circumference, and six fathoms up,
Bulg'd at its sides, in form like as a cup,
Less at its base ; and round about the same
There spread an horizontal ardent flame,
So great the heat, that not a soul could dare
Approach within ten fathoms of the flare :
And on the rim of this most mystic vase—
One fathom high—a bluish flame arose,
Which shed an incense o'er the inner part ;
And warders stood thereon, each with a dart,
Fierce in their look and ghastly in their mien :
And farther down a girdle, red and green,
Of furious fire, revolved around the shroud
Which hid the gods† from the obsequious crowd :
And where, within, the arbitrators stay'd
For one whole hour, intent upon the dead—
As to the burial of the god, and how
He should be welcom'd in the realms below ;—

<hr>

* Son of Chaos.   † Pluto and Apollo.

For 't was Apollo's wish that he should be
Receiv'd with pomp into eternity,
And urged the matter to the full extent,
Till Pluto graciously gave his consent.

*   *   *   *   *

The god,* now pleas'd, sent up a yellow shaft—
Which Boreas,† mighty wind, away did waft
Across th' unfathomable red abyss,—
And which in transit caused a fearful hiss.

When Vulcan, seeing, alone, the signal bound,
Re-beat his gong,—the vassal host around,
Quick as a flash of lightning, then upheld
Their polish'd dirks on high, and then re-yell'd !
The mighty magistrates, obeying the sound,
Inclined their heads, and knelt upon the ground :
The while, Apollo (and his mirthful throng)
Came forth, repeating the triumphant song—
" Hail, Pluto, mighty King !"—around him slung
His instrument of joy,—his eye relit
With his accustom'd dignity and wit.

Immediately, the cloud collaps'd and fled,
And he, the lord of death, appeared glad :
He stood erect, and, in the act of pray'r,
Pour'd forth his orisons into the air :
His pow'rful speech made all the host afraid,
And instantly his mandates were obey'd :
He spoke but once—his chariots were at hand,
And round about him his attendants stand,—
Each in apparel dazzling to the sight,—
Their wings outspread in readiness for flight.

* Pluto.   † The north wind.

Then Pluto look'd about the torrid space,
Stepp'd in his chariot with a kingly grace,
And rais'd his beam, full half a ton in weight :
When (pointing to his own imperial seat,
Which stood upon a mount encompass'd round
By awful chasms and unstable ground,)
He gave the word—the trumpets shook the vast
With the outpourings of their mighty blast !

  *   *   *   *   *

The clouds divided, and the train pass'd through ;
And now the multitude shout out anew—
" Hail, Pluto, mighty King !" great was the noise.
The quivering earth dissolved into the skies.
Above, below, around, was void and dark
For one whole day, until a vivid spark
Of crimson flame—in form a serpent's sting—
Shot forth towards the mountain of the king,
And struck the base of the imperial throne,
Which shook with awe ; and all the earth did groan :
A flash of light lit up the horrid zone ;
The atmosphere 'came full of monster frogs,
Of winged porcupines, and howling dogs.

     ———

CANTO THE SECOND.

Now when Apollo from the cloud came forth
He took his chariot, drove towards the north,
From whence he came ; while Boreas stretched a
   limb,
And sent a whirlwind to accompany him
Back to the regions of the world above :

But on his way he stay'd beneath a grove,
Of moderate magnificence, and where,
With solemn grandeur, dwelt—in midway air—-
The Empress of the palls,* despair, and woe,
Who greeted him with a most graceful bow.
She saw the god was mournful in his look,
Surmised his errand, and, in haste, betook
Her folio, and, with her refulgent shaft,
Made (as he spake) a brief but careful draft
Of his demand. Apollo (whose delight
Defied conception), seeing the marv'lous flight
With which her shaft had plann'd the burial-rite,
Declared his acquiescence ; and with voice—
Conceived by him most suited to her choice—
Which made the solemn goddess' heart rejoice,
Demanded when and what the hour would be
That Bacchus should go down t' eternity.
She straightway answered him, and meetly named—
" Within an hour the god shall be embalmed ;
And on the morrow, as the sun goes down,
The car of death shall through the gulf be drawn.
Five hundred horse," she said, " of equal size,
Shall form the vanguard to the realm of sighs ;
From every horse a rein shall concentrate,
And mighty Hercules† shall drive in state ;
For he, alone, hath strength at his command
To grasp the giant bridle in one hand ;
Whilst with the other he upholds his beam,
And sends the silver lash forth with a scream :

* Libitina, goddess of funerals.
† A son of Jupiter, remarkable for his wondrous strength and numerous
exploits.

J

The goddess Mors* shall join the funeral train,
Close followed by the nymphs, arranged in twain;
Whose sun-brown'd faces shall be draped with care,
Their bodies plaited immortelles shall wear;
At each one's side a tabour shall be slung,
Which, beaten, will enhance the mournful song."
  This said, Apollo wing'd his car again,
And drove direct to where the god was lain;
There he beheld his Daphne standing by,
Still venting forth her grief with moistened eye
(The faithful goddess, charitable queen,
Beside poor Bacchus' form a day had been):
Her soul was sad, her lips refusèd food;
Yet, like a guardian-angel, there she stood
Contemplating what ought or might be done
With the cold corpse; whilst her fair lord had gone
Down to the chambers of the mighty god.
He now saluted her with courtly word—
" O Daphne! thou art dear t' Apollo's heart;
Look up, O nymph! and list whilst I impart
Pluto's commands with reference to the dead!"
She heard his voice, and rais'd her heavy head;
So pleased to see her gentle lord return
She ceas'd her tears, but did not cease to mourn:
Her auburn tresses answered to the breeze
Which goodly Zephyrus† sent by slow degrees. —
Presuming that her nearly-fainting form
Might be sustain'd and succourèd from harm:
But ere she 'd time to utter forth a sound,
A mighty rumbling shook the very ground!

---

* The goddess of death.   † The west wind.

They turn'd and saw advancing on the plain
Meek Libitina, and her sombre train ;
Then in an instant they were mute and calm,
Whilst the black host proceeded to embalm
The still fresh-coloured, robust shape of him
Who now had ceased to be—like as a dream.
(The fragrant perfume of the embalming-herbs,
The death-impregnant atmosphere absorbs :
Round and about, the vines were still in bloom ;
But all a mournful posture did assume :
The glassy-bumpers ev'n appearèd dull,
And for awhile their liquors turn'd to gall :
The azure sky was totally obscur'd ;
But Sol himself was not to be immured,—
He stay'd, as 'twere within two leagues of Earth,
And penetrated through the halo-girth
Intensely red and hot, to mark his love
For the fall'n god, the earthly friend of Jove :)
This * done, the gloomy host returned below
Unto the palace of the queen of woe ;
Where preparations were going briskly on,
To bury Bacchus at to-morrow's sun,—
The going-down thereof, she thought the proper course
For the interment of his giant corpse.
'Twas coming night,—the eve of that sad day
When all the starry gods would come to pay
Their last respects unto the lifeless clod,
In form of man, now lying upon the sod,—
" And Daphne !" said the nymph, " to watch alone
(Save the companionship of the pale moon),

---

* The embalming of the body of Bacchus.

Throughout those dreary hours without a soul? * * *
Oh, stay, my love, and o'er me have control."
This, said to Apollo, fired his sapient brain :
His love for Daphne nought could now restrain !
(So "in the midst of life we are in death ;"
And "all is vanity" the preacher saith.)—
Apollo stay'd, and slept upon the field,
And nursed his love as mothers nurse a child.

Now, Leo's nights were short, so day came on ;
Aurora * blush'd to see the beauteous moon :
But she †—the virtuous angel of the night,
Succumb'd ; and thus withdrew her silvery light.

Prodigious Sol then soared into the main ;
And with him soared Apollo's tuneful strain,—
His prayer in song—so pithy and so sweet,
Ne'er fail'd t' imprint its influence on the great
Celestial magnates, nobles of the air.
But Bacchus' death nigh drove them to despair !
They knew not that the god was lying dead,
Until Apollo (not in vain) had pray'd
For them to come and join the ritual :
Nor for a moment did they deign t' recall
The disappointment when they all went down,
To Bacchus' cry, and found the god was gone :
They sought for no excuse, but came at once—
Garb'd in their glory—through the vast expanse
Of heav'n, and 'lighted on the plain, whereat
The great musician and fair Daphne sat.

First, Jupiter (Jehovah of the skies,
Whose silver hair, in ringlets, reach'd his thighs ;

---

* Goddess of the morn.   † The moon.

And round his waist, most splendid to behold,
Were jointed girdles wrought of solid gold,
And golden shoes, protectors of his feet,
Enhanced the splendour of his manly gait :
He grasp'd a sceptre sixteen feet in length ;
Himself next to great Hercule's in strength :
Superb in mien, and venerably grand ;
Whose eye no mortal goddess could withstand.)
Arrived ; as he advanced, six feet of ground
Escaped his tread at each successive bound :
Twelve feet he stood ; his hair fell o'er his brow,
And from his chin a nevious beard did flow :
Towards the soil his feather'd limbs inclined :
His countenance bespoke a gentle mind :
(Once the poor god, now dead, implored his aid ;
Who smote the fount and Bacchus' thirst was stay'd.)
Seen in the distance, thundering as he came,
He look'd a god of most uncommon frame !
Poor Daphne shook to see his wondrous form :
Her noble blood began to mingle warm ;
But pale and circumspect she did remain,
Impress'd with awe, her eyes straight to the plain
Upon th' incumbent god,—whose time was come
To be removed into the dismal tomb.

　　Next to great Jupiter, came Mercury,—
His flesh as smooth and white as ivory,—
Though not so tall, as handsome as the one
Already there, and sadly looking on ;
Yet Mercury is both great in stature, and
Appear'd a lord possessed of much command
In the ethereal mansions ; nay—in speech
So eloquent—no other gods could match.

Then came his majesty the monarch Mars,
In crimson robes inwoved with diamond stars ;
Robust and hale the god of war appear'd,
With azure eyes ; with saffron colour'd beard :
In fight, no other god could dare offend ;
And seldom did the monarch condescend
To make acquaintanceship with others, for
He proudly thought himself superior ;
Yet he, in token of his great regard
For him who lay upon the bruised sward,
Threw off his mask of pride, and came below :
With him he brought his unstrung golden bow,
To mark his rank and office in the skies ;
But here he stoop'd, and stooping yielded sighs,—
Griev'd to the heart to see poor Bacchus so :—
Him once so warm, but now as cold as snow.

That other belted god, mysterious being,
Saturnus came, and stood fourth in the ring
Which now began to encompass Bacchus round ;
His hair jet-black, his aspect most profound :
A purple garb hung loose around his loins,
To which his badge of honour meetly joins ;
His eagle eyes were now bedimm'd with tears,—
He mourn'd for him he'd known a thousand years ;
And more than once his sighs were loud indeed :
In his sad countenance the heart could read
Th' amount of sorrow his grave breast contained ;
His strength of mind increasing tears restrained ;
And to denote his senatorial rights,
Brought down with him his seven satellites :
He, punctual as to time, was at his post,—
There murm'ring forth " O Bacchus, Bacchus, lost

The Georgian Planet, stripling* of the air,
In grand habiliments forth did repair
Unto the scene of grief; not over tall,
Yet bore the image of his master, Sol;
He saw the corpse, and plainly did foreshow
(Though stratagem allowed no tears to flow)
His feelings at the sight of death; but he—
Child of the skies—bore up courageously:
He (with his satellites—six beauteous lads,
Esteemèd much among the greatest gods—
Attending in their robes of lightish-blue,
'Terwoven with fine gimp of golden hue),
Attract'd the grave attention of old Mars;
Who hail'd him as the " Herschel of the Stars,"—
And beckon'd him t' advance, and kiss'd his hand :
The stripling blushed ; he could not understand
Why, or wherefore, such favour should be shown
To one so young by one so olden grown ;
Yet felt much pleasure on being recognis'd,
Whilst more superior gods (as though despis'd)
Array'd in gorgeous dress, of greater growth,
And, in his estimation, greater worth,—
Stood silently and mournfully around,
Intent upon the death-inclosure mound.

Earth,† most profound, in her unfeigned grief—
Smote her bare breast ; her speech was very brief;
She felt a pressure on her noble heart,
But in the rite she took an ample part,—

---

* "Stripling" is intended to signify its more recent discovery in the heavens than that of the other planets.
† The World.

Survey'd the gulf down which the corpse would pass,
And lined its edges with resplendent moss :
Most modest, and most generous soul,
She'd oft contributed to Bacchus' bowl,—
Prolong'd his life in most abundant ease,
Until decrepitude besought release ;
And still regarded him as one of those
Whom she, herself, could least afford to lose :
" But he is gone ! and with his corpse a tear
Shall stray," said she, " upon the sinking bier ;
And when regenerated he shall rise,
Earth shall be first, for joy, to dim her eyes."

Revolving Venus, Empress of the globes,
Extremely beautiful, in purple robes,
Came now majestically o'er the sward ;
In rev'rence to the dead, spoke not a word :
Though, in her joy, her voice was like a lute,
She wept in silence, and remainèd mute :
Her rosy crown with jew'ls shone like the Sun,
And tipp'd her tear-drops as they trickled down :
On either side a Cupid, doubly fair,
Bore up the tresses of her golden hair ;
The Graces guarded her upon the plain ;
And fair Adonis held her diamond train :
Her shell-shaped chariot (rearward on the field)
Of ivory wrought, no eye had e'er beheld
More beautiful or more enchanting beams,
Carved in one solid mass—devoid of seams.

Behold Diana, goddess of the chase ;
Mark well her features, and her lovely face !
She, with dear Venus, set the world on fire
With love and beauty, which induced satire :

Fair daughter of great Jupiter, she stood—
Eyes fix'd upon the ground—in pensive mood ;
Her bow, her quiver, deer-skin on her breast,
Distinctly pointed her from out the rest.
Poor Actæon (youth, most skilful with the bow—
Whose eyes betray'd him, and led on to woe)
Beheld, by chance, the goddess in the lake ;
Dreamt not his own existence was at stake ;
But in an instant Fate, with double wrath,
Transform'd into a stag th' incautious youth ;
And there, upon the bank, before her face—
His end was wrought by his own dogs of chase.
(To contemplate his end we stand aghast ;
For dire indeed was the poor stripling's last !)
   Among the other goddesses and nymphs,
We scan the circle, and at once we glimpse
Good Agenora, most industrious child,
Laborious maiden on the barren wild ;
Who toil'd for ages, and ('twas not in vain)
Made a vast wilderness bear lovely grain :
She by Diana stood, meek, yet sedate,
And trespass'd not beyond her own estate.
   Aurora, lovely nymph with wings outspread,
Having heard with sorrow that the god was dead,
Came like a cloud across the purple field ;
And, as she swept along the air, did gild
With the reflection of her crimson folds
Hills, valleys, mountains, plains, and gorsèd wolds.
(O lovely nymph ! more lovely in the morn,
When o'er the heav'ns thy radiancy is borne ;
When thou, with magic touch, the gates unbar,
And bid to rest that struggling little star—

Last in the field of night, which fain would stay
To see the beauties of th' advancing day
But weak in its endeavours to withstand
The saffron firmament, holds forth its hand
To shield its face from the bedimming flood ;
And in its turn forsakes the neighbourhood
Of heaven.)   And now she 'lights among the gods :
To every one she, sweet enchantress, nods ;
And, calmly drawing her gorgeous mantle round,
Pores o'er the lifeless body on the ground.

 Four other goddesses, for virtue famed,
Who, for their sweet demeanour, should be named :
Minerva, Astrea, and Concordia, three ;
First, for her wisdom and sagacity ;
The second, for her justice much renown'd ;
And next, the third, for peace and concord found ;
The fourth, for loveliness, Hygeia stands,—
Health in her face, and garlands in her hands.

 Omphale, nymph beloved by Hercules ;
And Hero, " beauteous woman," came from Thrace.

 Besides all these, there came Historia forth :
Fair Ceres,* benefactress of the Earth :
Lubentia, cheerful goddess, draped her face,
And came with all her charms veil'd o'er with lace :
Fair Flora, graceful child, herself a flower,
Brought all the beauties from her fairy bower :
Pure Februa, who never once did feign
Her love to any, joined the mournful train.

 Now came high Juno, lovely queen of heaven,
August in form ; by whom were peacocks driven

---

* Goddess of agriculture.

Through the blue path which led unto the scene;
Her crown and sceptre graced her noble mien;
She, mother of great Mars, and Vulcan, too,
Bedoff'd her smiles, as solemnly she drew
Unto the place where stood the sorrowing nymphs,
And sigh'd whilst on the corpse she cast a glimpse.
    In the first rank the famed Cybele was;
(The spouse of Saturn, who gain'd such applause
For all his exploits in the heavenly space,—
Described before with those of equal race;)—
She, as fair Vesta, is the bounteous globe;*
And came arrayed in spring's delightful robe:
Her crown of tow'rs pointed to the skies,
Which proved a landmark for a thousand eyes:
Of many flow'rs her vestment bore the print,
. And charmed the eye with their impressive tint;
With her great key spring's treasures she lets loose,
And with a generous hand deals them profuse'.
    These† formed the host of mourners that were
        bidden,
Beneath the cloudless concave of great heaven,
To bear their witness to the last remains
Of him, who now was past all mortal pains.
(Though not a cloud that day‡ was ever seen,
Sol wore a halo, and look'd very dim,—
The only way the god could mark his love,
As through the heavens he slowly seem'd to move,
Towards the one who'd revelled in his ray,
And welcomed him at each successive day.)

---

* The earth.
† The superior and inferior deities and planets enumerated in the poem.
‡ Of the interment of Bacchus.

But now the hour was fast approaching when
They expected forth the sad and sombre train :
There stood Apollo, foremost on the plain,
To watch with his bewitching eyes, the vast
Terrestrial space.   At length he heard a blast,
Which Boreas bore towards th' assembled throng ;
And furthermore, he heard the mournful song,
As they advanc'd upon the wings of woe :
('Round and about the corpse tears freely flow,
For gods and goddesses, resplendent clad,
Turn'd deathly pale, and certainly look'd sad :)
Swift as the winds would bear them, on they came ;
In front a herald to proclaim the name
Of the deceasèd god.   " Behold," he said,
" This body here upon the field now laid,
Is that of Bacchus, the great god of wine,
Who till'd the ground, and rear'd the lovely vine ;
The great dictator of the heathen laws :
His numerous talents gain'd him much applause :
Wise, though lascivious, he to powèr grew ;
Was surnam'd Bassareus, and Iacchus, too :
Built many cities, and won victories :
The benefactor of societies :
Son of great Jupiter,—Semele's child,—
On whom, in early life, Silenus smil'd ;
And whom the nymphs embraced with filial love,
Through which they gain'd their access unto Jove :
Phœnicia's King,—his wisdom he unfurl'd ;
His subjects taught to navigate the world,
For which—and other exploits—thus shall he
Be grandly welcom'd to Eternity : "—
And then he blew his trumpet, call'd aloud—

" Bear witness to the deed, ye assembled crowd,
Whilst I the fallen god's remains enshroud."
   Then, as they alight upon th' adjacent ground,
Five hundred horse sent forth a trampling sound ;
And mighty Hercules was in the rear
(For not another god could bear the gear)—
High in the air, upon the funeral car ;
His helmet shining like a glorious star :
From his great beam a scream resound the skies
As they progress—swift as an eagle flies.
With him came Mors, who gave two heavy sighs ;
A hundred deaths she had attended to,
But never one like this—so fraught with woe !
Her vesture hanging in loose folds of black,
Her hair all straighten'd o'er her graceful back,
Betokened grief; she ne'er conceived to crave
Poor Bacchus for the dread and dismal grave :
No, no, 'twas he himself,—his great excess,
That brought upon the earth such dire distress :
Yea, had he been a little circumspect,
Another thousand years his brow may've deck'd ;
But his lascivious habits, silly god,
Brought him thus soon to grace the viny sod.
     *   *   *   *   *

Now to the grave !—a gulf six fathoms wide,
Six in its length, and straight on every side ;
Down which no eye doth dare to penetrate ;
For to the realm of sighs this was the gate :
Four cedar beams, exactly wrought to shape,
Lie, near each brink, across the dreadful gap ;
Four other beams of equal size extend
Towards the heav'ns, and centre in one end ;

To which a chain, wrought out of Ætna's fire,
Pass'd through an aperture a cubit higher
(Its length ten leagues, and polish'd every link);
One end in hell, and one upon the brink,
Upon the side whereat the funeral train
Would yield the corpse; there, on the sacred plain,
To be uplifted, and then gently swung
O'er the abyss!   Hark to the obit's song!
As on the sad procession wend their way,
In funeral paces, at the wane of day:
The sound increases as they, slower still—
Far on the plain, come o'er a gradual hill,
On which an arch built up with lovely pines—
Entwined with olives and selected vines—
Bore on its top a crimson flame, which 'rose
To light the cortége as it onward goes;
For now the sun was sinking fast below
The dark horizon of the western brow.

   'Tis now indeed a melancholy hour;
For, as they line the brink, they hear the roar—
The thunder of great Vulcan's mighty gong:
Besides, they hear, though faint, th' Infernals' song
Of joy; and there, as round the vault they stand,
Is heard the clamour of th' uproarious band
Let loose below, to revel at their will,
Till Mulciber shall bid them to be still.
Then suddenly up shot into the air
From out the gulf, a stream of yellow flare;
And then a sulph'rous cloud involved the pit,
In which a thousand infant demons flit,
Most wretched to behold; but joy for them,
And all the spirits who were waiting him—

The dead ! Now griev'd Apollo, standing near,
Waved his white rod (but waved it with a tear),
The signal to uplift the ponderous bier
Above the gulf. Below, a sound arose,
As round the giant-axle slowly moves ;
Contracting, every turn, the clinking chain,
Which lifted Bacchus from the purple plain.

   *   *   *   *   *

When (as the body swung into the cloud)
Apollo struck his harp, the noble crowd
Of gods and goddesses their tabours rung,
And peal'd the requiem in most glorious song !
Said Hercules, who almost long'd to die—
When first the anthem broke into the sky—
(The corpse was then descending the abyss,)
" Oh, give me death, and bury me like this !"
He doff'd his helmet (noble was his brow),
And as a child the hero seemèd now ;
For while he listen'd to th' harmonious flow
Of sound, unmatch'd on earth, his heart did leap.
And Pan was there with his melodious pipe ;
Who—god of woods, of shepherds, most divine—
On this occasion made his genius shine,—
His reed he blew with such delightful force,
That Hercules rejoic'd, so did his horse.
 Apollo's nine companions * there with him,
Enhanced the grandeur of the mournful hymn :
Fair Terpsichore look'd sad, but sang most sweet,
And timed most gracefully the poet's feet :

    * Daughters of Jupiter. The Muses

Euterpe, too, th' inventor of the flute,
Was only rivall'd by fair Clio's lute :
And Calliope's sweet enchanting voice,
Made heart and soul and flesh rejoice :
The songs of Polyhymnia were so dealt,
Gods, great and small, turn'd gravely as they knelt
To see from whence the melody arose :
She heeded not,—and on her singing goes
Till e'en the ground beneath them, where they stood,
Seem'd to give ear : and Mars was much subdued.
Erato, Thalia, blest Urania, and
Melpŏmene the grave, complete the band,
Who came from far their tuneful aid to lend ;
And with their songs their prayers for Bacchus send
To Him, the Sovereign of continual death,
Of woe, of mis'ry, and eternal wrath !

❋   ❋   ❋   ❋   ❋

For one whole hour the requiem did not cease ;
Its words, interpreted, were writ as these—
" O mighty king !   O Pluto, lord of hell !
Extend thy grace to his departed soul :
Receive his corpse, and furnish it with breath,
That he may revel in the realms of death :—
So that our loss may be thy kingdom's gain."
A pause ensued : and then a dreadful cry
Came up the grave, which rent the gloomy sky.
With it arose a wave of crimson flame
Up straight towards a cloud that cover'd them :
Which shaped itself into a feather'd beam,
And wrote upon the cloud, thus : " Bassareus lives !"
    To their wits' end the gods and goddesses

Were driv'n : they scan the cloud and there behold
The marv'lous scrip in letters of bright gold :
Anon they gazed, until it vanishèd,
And gods conferr'd like men astonishèd.

They now resolved to wend their way from earth ;
Some East, some West, some South, and others North :
Their minds, indeed, impressed with mighty things ;
Such as did baffle all their reasonings.

As Hercules flew swiftly to the East,
Apollo and fair Daphne to the West,
Straight from the North great Boreas swept the plain,
And bore a portion of the mystic train
To the south region of the mournful height,
(For not a star had deign'd to shine that night,)—
Yea, all was dark.   Earth, Air, and Ocean, now
Were void.   Not so in the dread realms below :—
Where there were spirits—tens of thousands, fiends,
Whose shrieks were borne upon the various winds
Of hell ; and who with awful vengeance swore
That such should be for ever, evermore !
Where mountains labour in the trough of woe,
And topple over on the host below :
Where valleys lift themselves, and roll in waves :
Where grim idolaters rise from their graves
And walk the plains like skeletons of death,
Imparting oaths at each receding breath ;
Whose tongues hang down upon their fleshless breasts,
And waste their foam like over-burthen'd beasts.

But there were, also, those grandees of state ;
And in their midst that mighty Autocrat,
The Governor of all therein ; and he
Unbarr'd the gate of immortality :

K

While Vulcan, in attendance on the god,
Had watch'd his master, and observed his nod :
Towards the corpse he went, and breathed one
    breath,—
When Bacchus 'rose, and doff'd his robe of death !

      *   *   *   *   *

This was the moment when upwent that cry
Which, as 'twas said, had rent the gloomy sky :
This was the moment that the fiery waves
Wrote on the cloud above them—" Bassareus lives ! "
And this the hour that Earth, and Air, and Sea,
Was one vast waste of transient misery !
When all the gods and goddesses were thrown
Into a state of tremulous concern,
And took themselves to flight, each one their way,
To write their records of the dismal day.
    Now, Proserpine,* she, Pluto's august queen,
Was present to augment the novel scene :
(No goddess, Pluto—though his power was great—
Could e'er induce to share his vast estate ;
He, vex'd, enraged, deformed, despised, went forth,
Stole Proserpine, and sunk into the earth ;
Which deed, great consternation then provoked
Among the Virgins, where he 'rose : they look'd,
But 't was in vain, for suddenly they 'd gone
Down to the caverns of the mighty one.)
She saw poor Bassareus lift his ruffled head,—
Observ'd his deathied cheeks flush to a red :
And saw his eyes revolve, as 'round he gazed
Upon the crowd, and stood—as though amazed—

      * Wife of Pluto.

Contemplating with evident deep thought
The strange transfiguration which was wrought.
   Forth Pluto stepp'd, and, holding out his hand,
Embraced the god.   *   *   *   The then surrounding
    band
Of wondering magnates, vie* and send abroad—
"LONG LIVE GREAT BASSAREUS!"   "HAIL OUR
    NEW-BORN GOD!"
Then all the multitude join'd in the song,
And ceasèd not, till Vulcan beat his gong;
When to the palace the great concourse went;
And on the mount, where dwelt th' omnipotent
Unmerciful, great god, to light the way
Ten thousand torches flamed towards the sky;
And all within, and out, was revelry.
Uninterruptedly, for nine whole days
The carnival endured: a fervent blaze—
Meanwhile continuing—cast a melting heat
Upon the host assembled round the seat
Of Pluto. But poor Bacchus grew afraid,†—
He being an alien in the land of dread:
When first he saw the gloomy element,
His heart forsook him, and much tears he spent;
When first he heard the thunderings of hell,
He beat his breast, and cursed his living soul;
When he beheld the fiends fly 'cross the course,
He stamp'd the ground, and grumbled with remorse;
When at a furnace-heat the winds did blow,
More sad, dejected, did poor Bassareus grow;—
His anguish now became so great, he foamed,

    * With their tremendous shouts.
    † Here follows Bacchus' agony.

Inclined his head towards the ground, and moaned:
Now raved aloud for that he loved on Earth,
To cool his tongue and wash his frothy mouth:
Then shook his head, and swung it like a plumb,
Reviling bitterly his mother's womb:
Discomfited, he sent a piteous cry * * *
(Which all the host interpreted for joy.)
And roar'd aloud—" Ye gods of hell, be damn'd
(The more he cried less did they understand.)
Upon his ears their hideous chorus dwelt;
And as the direful strain of discords swell'd
He roll'd himself upon the heated earth;
(They misconstrued it into signs of mirth;)
Then bit his flesh, and pluck'd his bearded chin;
Besought the gods to disembowel him !
(But more and more the tumult did increase:
Awhile he swore—they sent into the space
Their boisterous shouts in honour of their king,
And unto Bacchus tuned their welcoming.)
Yes—he, poor god, grew more and more depress'd :
His temples swoll'n, and every joint oppress'd
With pain intense, he cried—" None so distress'd
As I, * * * none half so wretched, * * *
        none so lorn, * * *
Not one so miserable was ever born !"

Great Pluto, seeing the god most sorely wroth,
(For on his bearded chin there lurk'd the froth,)
Said unto him—" O Bassareus ! why so sad ?"
Pray doff thy sorrow, and uplift thine head,—
Behold the grandeur of my Palestine :
On yonder mountain, next in rank to mine,

And in the clouds, a castle I will raise,—
In which (my will is) thou shalt pass thy days,
And there remain, till Jupiter shall call,
Shall call thee hence unto the world of Sol!"
(These words electrified the mournful god,
Who rubbed his eyes, and scann'd the multitude.)
Continued Pluto : "Thine the fault shall be,
If thou dost not enjoy felicity :—
For in thy mansion vassals thou shalt have ;
A guard of honour, powerful and brave,
Shall be, Friend Bassareus, at thy own command ;
And in my senate thou, at my right hand,
Shall hold the sceptre of unrighteousness ;
Thy chief attendants shall be Lachesis,
And Clotho, and their sister Atropos ; *
Those noted creatures of fatality :
And with them, as companions, there shall be
Megæra, Alecto, and Tisiphone, †
Endowed with gifts most suitable to thee :
And, furthermore, to enhance thy glory here,
My orders shall go forth to Mulciber,
To forge a chariot of Corinthian brass,
Of great dimensions, that thou mightest pass
About the regions of thy residence
With solemn grandeur, and magnificence.

    *   *   *   *   *   *

As now when Bassareus, with derision, smiled,

---

* The three Fates.
† The three Furies.
NOTE.—It is the author's intention if spared, and his friends—sub-scribers to this little work—appreciate his motive) to represent, in a subsequent poem, "The Resurrection of Bacchus,"—his return and glorious reception upon Earth, etc.

And grew, dissemblingly, more reconciled,
He clench'd his hands and 'rose a cubit higher
(Red as the elements that raged with fire),
And turned his sweating face towards the sky :
Unheeding the vast crowd's tumultuous cry,
His lips, with much emotion, seemed to move :
At last he thunder'd out this prayer to Jove,—
"O Sovereign Jove ! lord, god of air and earth,—
Thou benefactor, guardian of my youth,—
Behold my sorrow, and mine agony !   *   *   *
Sustain me, Jove, in my adversity !   *   *   *
My flesh is melting with the dreadful blaze
Revolving round the vast infernal space :
My hunger and my thirst 's unbearable ;
The noise of hell—most incomparable !—
From which, O Jove ! with Pluto intercede,
That of these torments Bacchus may be freed :
And if 't is possible, O Jupiter !
With all thy majesty in Earth and Air,
Thy wit, thy wisdom, and unrivalled power ;
Whose eloquence of speech, whose well-earn'd store
Of heav'nly honours, none can e'er surpass,—
Speak thou to Pluto, that I may repass
Through that great gulf, back to those orient plains,
There bask again among those teeming vines ;—
There——" but as he spake this word* (and 't was his
    last !)
Loud thunders clapp'd, and lightnings rent the Vast
Tornadoes, furiously the plains career'd ;
And all the host of hell aghast appear'd !

* The word " there," at the beginning of same line.

Now Bassareus cried ; tears mingled with his sweat ;
He lash'd his body, and defined a threat,
And coupled with it a most horrid oath ;
Which Pluto could not bear.   So, in his wroth,
He turn'd an Enemy ; and, with disdain,
Commanded all the Elements to rain
A torrent of red flame !—Down came the flood !
The merc'less fluid, mingled with the blood
Of tens of thousands (in an instant slain),
Rush'd like an ocean o'er the smoking plain.

       *   *   *   *   *

   *   *   *   *   *

From his high towers—the deluge, Pluto saw.
The dissolution of the host below
Chang'd not his countenance.   A thousand times
This haughty monarch (and for lesser crimes
Than those of Bassareus') scourged the land with fire,
Durst any magnate to provoke his ire.
Said he to Proserpine—" Lift I my hand,
Ten thousand demons are at my command :
Burn I as many every day, nay hour,
Lift it again, and lo ! ten thousand more
Are at my feet. * * * Weep not, O Proserpine !
No such destruction shall be ever thine ;
Nor Vulcan's fate : he, Pluto's chief, shall dwell
For ever in those glorious realms of hell.
   Nox,* ancient creature, shall for ever find
My heart in favour, and my edicts kind :
Though dark her ways, her manners I approve,—
She makes no prayers to Jupiter or Jove,—

        * The goddess of Darkness.

And next to Proserpine doth share my love ;
Contented, amiable, and circumspect,
The good old goddess, Pluto shall protect.
    Nor giant Charon,* constant at his post,
Conductor of the dead from coast to coast ;
Though rude his mien, him will I not despise ;
Him will I shelter from the flaming skies.
    My Judges, also, for their integrity,
Shall know no sorrow, nor adversity.
    Nor Cerberus,† my faithful, at the gate
(For ever ready to defend my state),
Shall never die, shall never lack my care
Whilst hell is hell, and Pluto master there !

* The ferryman of Hell.   † Dog with three heads.

A Poem, in Romance.

IN SIX CHAPTERS.

⸺

JANE HOLLYBRAND;

OR,

VIRTUE REWARDED.

⸺

BY

EDWARD EDWIN FOOT.

Jane Hollybrand; or, Virtue Rewarded.

CHAPTER THE FIRST.

I.

In yonder vale,—famed for its genial mould,
Its pastoral beauties, and rare grains of gold,*—
There, 'neath the shelter of a peasant's cot,
A pair of rosied cheeks was the fair lot
Of young Jane Hollybrand ; who had to toil,
To cook potatoes ; cauliflowers to boil ;
To scrub and clean the inside † oaken floor ;
To watch and feed the chickens at the door ;
To see the drowsy pig cried not in vain ;
To cheer in summer-time, or winter's reign,
Her loving father.   On returning home
From his day's work, she 'd say :—" Come, father,
      come."
And, with an angel's voice, so clear, so sweet—
" The supper's ready, father, take your seat."
    Alas ! her mother, Death had stol'n away
Just when 't was needed most that she should stay
For her child's good.   The poor man's heart was rent :
The twilight hour was regularly spent
In reading godly books ; wherein he sought
The Holy One, for help : then was he taught

---

* Corn.   † Inner room.

That sacred saying—life is but a span !
And then he'd sigh, and well he might, poor man.
   Twelve years of sweet conjugal happiness,
Had made their little home a paradise,—
'Til that grim monster stretch'd his deathy hand,
And marr'd the pleasures of George Hollybrand.
Great must, indeed, have been the father's grief ;
But gaining faith—through pray'r, he found relief.
He taught his darling with a father's care
To spell, to read, to write ; to be aware
Of certain youths ; who, from the village, found,
Their way unto the cottage-hallow'd ground.

II.

About this thatch-roof'd dwelling, so remote,
A blackbird chirped from its tiny throat
Its rural anthem ; and for this Jane gave
The brown-bread crumbs. she'd made a rule to save.
   So came the pretty robin-redbreast, too,—
(Oh ! that the world was half so good and true,)
She from the leaded window-sill would pick
With birdlike aptitude—so wondrous quick—
The frugal fragments of Jane's surplus store ;
Haste to her offspring, and return for more:
Sometimes the pretty creature chirp'd in vain,
But not when Jane could spare a crumb or grain.
   Throughout the months of April, May, and June,
Forth came the cuckoo, and chimed out his tune
Upon the sky-branch of the apple-tree ;
There, unmolested, perch'd he merrily :—
O ! happy favourite, of the wingèd host,

Where dost thou dwell—inland? or on the coast?—
Or in some dreary cave, where all is night,—
Belike earth's chaos ere God gave the light?
Say—whither shall imagination trace
Thy magic form ; to hear thee chime with grace
Thy rare ding-dong harmonious voice :
Oh ! tell us, tell us, that we may rejoice
In thy long absence,—that we may obtain
A fancied hearing of thy heav'nly strain :
Ah ! thine, indeed, must be a cherub's throat :
Who taught thee singing, blest one? or, by rote,
Didst thou, thy pretty self, improve the note
With such precision, that for miles around
Attentive list'ners hear thy twofold sound?
Thou art a sort of majesty in air,
Without a crown, without a kingdom's care :
When in July thou'st bidden all farewell—
Methinks I hear thee still in yonder vale ;
And long the joy to list thy voice again
When winter's past, and spring resumes her reign.

III.

Now in the spring-time of the coming year,
When in the south celestial hemisphere
Proud Horus mounted with increasing strength,
And each succeeding day had grown in length ;—
When April clouds their vernal drops had shed,
And bonny May had made all nature glad ;—
When that arch monarch had assail'd the moon,
And bade her quarter in the month of June ;—
Then in the garden, rearward of the cot,—

(A little oblong well-trimm'd fruitful spot,
Encompass'd round with hedge-row elder trees,)
Thenceforth would come the meek harmonious bees ;
There trip from plant to plant, from flow'r to flow'r,
A-gathering in their luscious golden store.
Some day, perchance, when Horus waxed warm,
The honied-host would sally forth and swarm :
Their movements little Jane would watch with care ;
Would call her father, and again repair
Towards the garden : then she knew full well
'T was time to fetch and swing the tinkling bell,
To save them winging down the orchard-dell.

  * * * * * *

 A stone-throw from this cot, where ran a stream
'Twixt mossy blocks of granite, there would gleam
The glowworm's beautiful and brilliant light,—
Whilst wandering in the silent lovely night,—
A living lantern in the darksome hours,
'Midst the green hawthorn and the wild-grown flow'rs,
For other insects of its kindred race,
Whose continent is but a little space.
 The rivulet (whose distant stream is heard
Careering on and on as though it fear'd
To lose its turn into eternity*—
To mingle in old Neptune's revelry,)
Is oft obscured by Nature's ambient sward ;
Oft check'd ; its reckless dance and frolic marr'd,
And turn'd aside to fill the farmer's pail
For breakfast, tea, and to make home brew'd ale.

    * The ocean.

IV.

Not far from here,* in this delightful vale,
The venerable squire's old mansion stood,
Surrounded by rich pasturage and wood ;
The squire, himself a rare good-natured gent,
Oft at this dwelling, hours of leisure spent ;
Would smoke his pipe, and not refuse to take
A crust of cottage bread, of honest† make :
The sweet demeanour of this youthful lass
Induced his " honour " to go there, and pass
A portion of his time in quiet talk—
In cautioning the damsel how to walk
Through life's rough path ; and whilst to him she'd
    listen,
Her face would crimson, and her eyes would glisten :
This frank old Englishman confess'd his pride
In stealing forth from home ; awhile to hide
From those gay gatherings within his halls,
Where fashionable folk make daily calls
(A-talking of the past, and coming balls,)
Their avocation,—there to bow and prate,
And worry nature in its last estate.

V.

It hap'd a gentle youth—a lordly heir
To vast domains—did annually repair
Unto this country-mansion, to renew
His pleasant visits to his uncle Prew :
The fair-hair'd stripling proved a welcome guest,

---

* The cottage.   † Unadulterated.

For there was something in his generous breast
Which won for him the universal mark
(From Bishop Butler,* to the parish-clerk,)
Of friendship—nay, the love of one and all :
The village-matrons, all were wont to call
Him " the young Squire ;" and as he pass'd their way
They'd call their daughters from the washing-tray,
Or spinning-wheel, or the old-fashion'd loom,
Or in the midst of scrubbing out a room,
Or at the pigs' sty—where they were intent
Upon the beast,† which paid the yearly rent :
And forth they 'd come—some with their naked arms ;
Some with their "wee-uns ;" some much skill'd in
        charms,—
For in most hamlets superstition reigns—
Where there is one at least, who sundry pains
Profess to cure by praying to the gods
With speechless lips, quaint motions, and queer nods ;
And some again, who 'd done their household needs,
Prim dress'd,—perchance a widow in her weeds,
Who 'd lost her dear-one by the hand of death ;
And others hastening, almost lacking breath.
    Some lazy tailors in a kitchen-shop,
Fond of a sight, from out the window 'd pop
Their uncomb'd heads of most peculiar shape,
With beards as bristly as the hog, or ape ;
Who for a shilling, breakfast, dinner, tea,
And aught beside, go forth and work the day
At some farmhouse (or at the village priest's),
Re-seating breeches, patching coats or vests.

' The imaginary) bishop of the diocese.   † The value of ·

And then the village cobbler drops his tool,
Throws down his spectacles, lifts from his stool
His grizzled visage ; not o'er fond of trade,
(Who often vows he wish'd the pick and spade
Had been his implements of industry,
Instead of hemp and wax machinery,)
He's not at all partic'lar what abuse
Accrues for keeping sons' or daughters' shoes
Much longer than he ought—he care ? not he !—
He's well inured to such-like trickery :
Come what there will, if there 's the slightest chance,
(Be 't funeral-weeping, or a wedding-dance,)
The faintest prospect—either facts or fibs—
Where there is hopes of friendship with some ribs
Of beef, sirloin, or rump, no matter which—
" The devil take the awl,"—not one more stitch
Will there be done that day ; on goes his best,
(Whate'er he 's got) and revels with the rest.
  The blacksmith, also, at the village forge,
(His handy-workman, or his own son George,)
Is not unlike the cobbler or the " snip,"
Just let him hear the cracking of a whip,
With rather more than usual dexterous hand,
He drops the sledge, and quickly makes a stand :
First gazes on the rider, then the horse,
The vehicle, if any ; and, of course,
Pulls half-way o'er his nose his old greas'd peak,*
(Tho' rough in manners, modest in his keep,)
Views well the fetlocks, and the horse's parts ;
His vete'nary skill in words imparts,—

---

* Peak of his cap', in making obeisance to the passer-by.

Consults his own, or his son George's mind,
And speaks the word according as he find   *   *   *

VI.

As there is always one* in every town
Who prattles much and takes transactions down,
Who smears the placard, then besmears the wall;
So there's in villages—however small—
A man whose wisdom he, perchance, conceives
Excels his neighbours', but himself deceives,—
A fellow who detests hard healthful work,
(By birth a Jew, or it may be—a Turk,)
Existing on his wit or tortuous brains,
Perhaps dishonest; and who takes sad pains
T' effect the purpose of his daily life—
The source of much contention and of strife;
In contradiction to all those who hap
To come in contact with the wily chap:
Here, there, then, when, and how; tells all he knows
And more.—at length it comes to blows:
Some fellow now detects his fraudful game,
Becomes combatable; at last with aim
Deals on his cheek, or breast, a direful shock!
The boaster 'turns not; dares, nor feigns to knock
His adversary: and so, disquieted,
He sneaks away; but not discomfited—
For when' 't is twilight there he is again
With pleasant features, but distorted brain,
Inducing some way-faring man† to cards;

* A news-monger, or " bill-sticker."
† Suppose him to be a pedler.

And whilst he shuffles, cuts, deals out, discards,
The knave has managed to get hold the ace
From out the pack; then with his wont grimace
Allows his trusty friend to win awhile
A few odd pence, and whilst he feigns a smile
He meditates to cheat him of his gold
Or silver coin; then dashes out so bold—
" Ace," " king," and " queen," (himself the " jack,")
And throws his comrade quite upon his back,
As 'twere ! The man, being sorely duped and " done,"
Picks up his sundry wares and travels on.   *   *   *

VII.

One sultry morning Lady Prew* grew faint :
So, to the cot, young Arnold† ran t' acquaint
His uncle ; for, as usual 'bout that hour,
He'd ta'en his pleasurable cottage tour :
Surprised, indeed, was he to see the youth !
" There's something wrong," he said ; " come, tell me
        truth ! "
So then the boy drew forth, and 'gan to say—
" Dear aunt is taken ill ; but uncle, pray
Don't be alarm'd : " when lo ! he 'spied (between
The quaint old settle, and a kind of screen,
Which hid a bed,) the lovely cottage queen :
Who, when she saw the gentle youth advance,
Had thither fled, and sought t' avoid his glance :
Her dark-blue eyes shone in that sombre light
Like glow-worms spangling in the depth of night :

---

* At Westonbury Hall, the "squire's" mansion.   † Arnold Mountjoy.

He saw !—he felt a smart impulsive move !—
And from that hour he sought t' improve his love.
The old man call'd the " lassie " forth and said
" 'There, Arnold, is she not a pretty maid ?—
She has the work of all the house to do,
Yet always clean : come, Arnold, we must go."
    The uncle dreamt not that his nephew's heart
Was smitten, wounded with love's keenest dart :
He little thought it—that henceforth this girl,
Of humble birth, would be so rich a pearl
To his " dear boy : " it never cross'd his brain
The youth so soon would wander there again ;
And there to press her tiny hand in his,
(The while implanting on her cheek a kiss,)
And leaving in that hand a valued ring,—
That when she saw 't she might, remembering
Some future day the giver, say— " Ah me !
How oft I've thought, and still shall think, of thee !
Thou art a treasure—O, thou beauteous gem !
I'll kiss thee now and think I'm kissing him :
Perhaps it 's but a dream, yet shall mine eyes
For e'er behold him in this pretty prize."

VIII.

Young Mountjoy now was nineteen years of age,
Susceptible to love, and prone t' engage.
His beauty, (as he call'd her) tall inclin'd,
Made such impression on his gentle mind
That he, with whom he went, wherever he stray'd,
Without disguise profess'd he lov'd the maid.
Three times, or more, within the cottage he

Improved the hour, and with solemnity
Pour'd forth his orisons.　(When all alone
He often 'd pray'd that Jane might be his own.)
　　Love's rosy tint flush'd her sweet cheeks and brow
As Jane beheld him ; yet she knew not how
Or why he lov'd her so : (but as she grew
She heard his voice in every breeze that blew.)
　　And now he kiss'd her cheek, and wept a tear
To think the hour of parting drew so near :
He thought (no doubt) at home there'd be no rest—
That dearest Jane would never be their guest ;
But still he thought—when many years are flown,
And I am lord and master of my own,
(Good Heaven willing it) my Jane shall then
Be welcom'd mistress at the old domain.

IX.

When George, returning home from work one day,
Saw at a distance by some ricks of hay
In the " eight-acre " field, close by the gate,
The well-known die,*—he paus'd : "as sure as fate,"
He said, " that 's my dear child !—what can it be?"
And hasten'd forward ; when she cheerfully,
Ran forth to meet him, say'ng " dear father look !"
At the same time she from her bosom took
A tiny parcel, which contain'd the ring ;
Unfolding it, and tip-toe whispering—
" For this I gave one little lock of hair,
And I must keep it with the greatest care
For Arnold's sake ; and, then besides all this,

* One of her poor mother's dresses.

He gave me such a loving, loving kiss,
And said—'When far and far away, that he
Should kiss that pretty curl and think 'twas me :—
The ring,' he said, 'was gold—of precious worth,
That he had priz'd it more than all the earth !'"
George seem'd amaz'd ; and speechless for awhile,
Sat brooding o'er it* on the gateway-stile :
A thousand things came flitting in his brain :
He thought, as thousands would, of her being slain
In childhood's sweet simplicity !
And pray'd to God to solve the mystery.
Thus he at once his cause to Heaven resign'd :
And Heaven as soon consoled his harass'd mind ;
For scarcely were his pray'rs (in silence said)
Gone forth on high, (whilst 'round his daughter
        play'd,)
When Jane this brief appeal t' her father made—
" Pray tell me, father, why you seem so sad ;
Oh ! was it wrong to take it from the lad ?
Forgive me, father, if I've done amiss :
He only press'd my hand and gave a kiss !"
Then George was comforted, and sped along,
Humming a kind of bass to Janie's song ;
But still he labour'd on in deep suspense—
Assur'd of this—that it would give offence
To all the folks† at Westonbury Hall ;
And thus it proved, for dreadful was the fall.—
Ambitious as they were, of rank and name
Nought ever shock'd the lady's tender frame
So much as this sad news. She found no rest ;

* His daughter's statement.   † The Prews.

Fell in a violent rage and smote her breast ;
Flew to her writing-desk, dipp'd pen in ink,
(Appear'd as tho' she thought it sin to think—
Ironic'lly exclaiming, ah ! ah ! ah !)
And wrote a lengthy note to Arnold's " pa."
Her fondest hopes, she said, were frustrated,
Which for so many years concentrated
In him. * * * God never bless'd them with a
        son ;
So she, it seems, had calculated on
A son-in-law, in Arnold ; but alas !
This hope had fled.   (Not like the blade of grass,
Which in the summer-time for lack of rain
Decays and dies, whilst there comes up again
One equally as rare when clouds recruit,
And shed their globules down to its root.
Nor like the corn-crops yellowing in July,
Slain by the reaper 'neath an August sky,
For there again shoots up, of equal worth,
Some other esculent to gladden earth.
No !—Arnold 's living ; yet for ever dead ;
His name is spoken, but with constant dread :
No longer shall he lift the wine-cup there,—
Ne'er more be welcom'd as the " lordly heir.")

                        X.

To Rollingate,* flew swift, as flew the mail,
From Westonbury Hall, the direful tale.
Lord Mountjoy donn'd his spectacles and read !
Then for a moment scratch'd his hoary head—

---

* The seat of Lord William Mountjoy :—Arnold's father.

Inclined to think it never could be true,
And half-inclined to doubt dear Lady Prew.
But never could his lordship entertain
The least degree of wrath, nor yet disdain,
Towards his son ;—"no ! time, alone, will prove
The best dictator of dear Arnold's love,"
He said—and thus : " I'll wait my boy's return,
And from his lips the secret try to learn."
    " Love," said Lord William, " is a desperate dart,
Not easily extracted from the heart ;
Wherein once seated, whether good or ill,
Retains possession—come who, or what will :
It is the buckler of the youth at sea,
The beam of war which gains the victory :
The soldier's hope : the banner of the soul :
The great consoler, and the Christian's bowl.
Where 's the proud bachelor who 'll dare to say
He never lov'd a damsel in his day?
Or where 's the spinster, when she heaves a sigh,
Can tell of none for whom she once could die ?"

XI.

When Arnold Mountjoy bade the Prews farewell,
It jarr'd the elder-ears, as doth the knell
Of some departed child—lov'd, but too well.
Alas ! he's gone : the door is clos'd, and fate
Had made the Prews the most disconsolate
Of creatures.   Yes, that morn, that wretched morn,
The lady cried ; the squire, he felt forlorn ;
And poor Miss Prew, she doubly sad as they,
Could not refrain from weeping bitterly.

As Arnold cross'd the park, he 'spied the smoke
Uprising through the branches of the oak,—
A noble tree, whose sturdy limbs had kept
The little cottage shelter'd on the left,—
Which spread its foliage o'er the gable end,
And frown'd, or would, on whom who dared t' offend
That little sacred dwelling-place of Jane.
And, furtherward, he turn'd and saw the lane
Which led from thence and thither to the cot ;
In front of which a small triangle spot,
(Where April "golden-cups,"* and daisies vie
To lure the trav'ler, or the tourist's eye,)
Was fenc'd with stones, crust from Earth's surface
      wrung ;
The fence was broad, and taper'd to make strong :
Three unwrought beams were set within the close,
With cords out-stretch'd, to dry the linen clothes :
There, he beheld—whom he admir'd the most,
Going 'round the inclosure ; then from post to post,
She skipp'd along, and seem'd attentively
Engaged in ranging out the drapery.
Now, stopping at a roadside shingle-gate,
He invented an excuse t' interrogate
An husbandman, in the immediate field,—
The nature of the soil, and of its yield ;
The owner of the land ; and whose the mill,
From whence the water-course which turn'd its wheel.
Receiving in reply the man's best wit,
Until he saw his pretty angel flit ;

---

* A pretty yellow flower, which generally abounds in Meadlands.

Then, unperceiv'd, he kiss'd his hand, and thrust
It forth towards the cot, pray'ng heaven's gust
Might waft it o'er; and with it went a sigh,—
His last adieu! and turn'd away his eye.

XII.

At noon, the coach* had yet twelve leagues to run:
The air grew chilly, and dark clouds begun
To form a leaden mass: entirely hid
Was he,† who in the morn 'rose round and red:
A dreadful storm was evidently near;
And distant rumblings fell upon the ear:
Yon wary sheep were gath'ring in a hav'n,
A shelter'd nook: the wind had now aris'n,
And boist'rously swept o'er the open-plain:
The sullen-featured clouds dispersed their rain
Tempestuously; and all around was gloom:
Increasing murm'rings in th' ethereal room,
And the first streak, shot thro' the sombre-rent,
Disturb'd an inside lady-occupant,
Who sought for sympathy from those without:
Th' affrighted horses fain would turn about;
But there's no help, no refuge from the storm
Until they gain'd "old Antrobus's farm—"
About three miles: when there the drenching-drops
Combin'd the gale, and bent the grainéd-crops:
Fork'd flittings quiver'd through the mournful vast;

---

* Which passed through the village of Westonbury, (situated about two
miles from the "Hall,") where Arnold had "book'd" himself for his journey
home.
† The Sun.

Th' inured coachman even sat aghast ;
For Heaven's artill'ry now had vollied forth
A deaf'ning roar,—which shook the stable earth.
    At length the storm subsides ; the clouds disperse ;
The welcome orb afresh begins t' immerse
The varied herbage, and the waving folds ;
Encompassing the furze and heathery wolds :
And all was calm again—save one poor soul,
Whose head still rang with the last thunder-roll.

XIII.

The beam of day had kiss'd th' horizon's pate,
Ere Arnold reach'd the lodge at Rollingate.
His anxious mother, most expectant grown,
Went forth to meet him o'er the verdant lawn :
As he advanc'd she hasten'd onward, and
Another instant join'd the mutual hand.
She saw the storm his garb had disarranged,
And bade him quickly get his garment changed :
For at the festive-board, the guests were there
Awaiting him, with simultaneous care.
When now the mother introduced her son
The guests saluted him,—as should be done.
In the meantime Lord William, lit with joy,
Held high the goblet, and embraced his boy !
And said "come Arnold, my belovèd son,
Sit thou on my right hand." The feast went on ;
The silver tankard circled round the hall,
And knights and fair-ones quaff'd the radiant bowl.
Thus the blithe evening ; (But that " cottage queen "
Still haunted Arnold 'midst the dazzling scene.)

Behold those weapons pensile on the walls,—
Huge carbines, fraught of yore with deadly balls ;
Shields, bucklers, swords, rough usage seem'd to show,
And batter'd helmets point the mortal blow.
Their battle-work was long since nobly done :
And those who wielded them, ah ! long since gone :
There also hung the pictures of the fray,
And him who won the laurels of the day :
He,* brave—though young—subdued the blazing fort;
Trusted in God, and—trusting—fought unhurt :
Return'd from war, with the surrender'd sword,
The king endowed him with a rich reward :—
He stoop'd a Baronet, and 'rose a " Lord."
His country eulogised him, without bounds,
And gave him, also, forty-thousand pounds ;
With which Lord William purchas'd the estate,—
The old manorial mansion,—" Rollingate."

  The guests had gone, about the midnight hour,
In various chariots, and the feast was o'er.

XIV.

As Lady Mountjoy was so doting kind
(Of calm demeanour, and of gentle mind,)
To her dear Arnold—him, her only son,
Whate'er he wish'd for, said : and it was done.
Too well she lov'd him, ever cross to speak ;
Or e'er t' upbraid him for his boyish freak.†
But Arnold's father felt that it was fraught
With disadvantage, and conceived (he thought)

---

* Arnold's father.   † As reported in Lady Prew's alarming letter.

An efficacious plan : matured the same,
Thus started Arnold on the road to fame.
At Court, Lord William's influence was used.
(A favor ask'd by him was ne'er refused ;
If that, solicited, could granted be,
Granted it was, and ever readily.)
So, for his son, h' obtain'd a post, at once—
In the legation, at the Court of France.
    In time, conversant with diplomacy,
He grew in favor,—e'en 'mong Royalty.
In Russia, Prussia, Austria, and in Spain,
The friendship of proud courtiers he did gain :
In India, China, Turkey, and at Rome,
A kind reception made him feel at home.
With great success he fill'd his place of trust,
In all transactions amiable and just,
His volubility and generalship
Soon gain'd a most distinguish'd consulship,
At one of Europe's gay commercial ports,
Where sovereigns frequent, and where wealth resorts :
Known by his genius, gentleness, and wit,
Where sat the monarch, close did Arnold sit ;—
A proud position, certainly, for one
Who had so young such reputation won.

XV.

Now, Arnold Mountjoy, tall, of handsome gait,
Had grown more pow'rful as he grew in height :
Erect he stood full seventy inches high :
His strength of arm enabled him to vie
At continental games successfully :

Where fair-ones frequented their praise to yield—
To him who won the honors of the field—
There Arnold found himself, and bore away
Full oft the prizes of the gamesome day.
But he, withal those pleasures at command,
Could not forget the home of Hollybrand ;
And nightly visions oft recall'd the spot ;
As oft, in dreams, he saw the little cot,
Wherein he trusted there did still remain
Whom he would call (and hoped) his " virgin Jane."

XVI.

It happen'd now, when fifteen years had flown,
That Arnold's parents, both were—dead and gone !
And he became sole master of his own,—
Inheritor of all his father's wealth.
Thus then, the son, being dubious of his health,
Bethought himself—to England I'll return ;
And there, my duty shall be first to learn
Whether old Hollybrand, of modest mien,
Is still protector of that "cottage queen :"
And she in beauty, virtue, now the same
As when she set my bosom in a flame !
If so, she still must be her father's joy,
And still dependent on his mere employ ;
Still scrubs the floor, and feeds the drowsy sow,
While George, himself, is toiling with the plough :
" Ah ! (Arnold said—whilst wond'ring if 't were so)
Six moons from now I trust in God to know."
This said, h' announced his firm resolve to go.

XVII.

Alas! grim Death, at Westonbury Hall,
Had number'd two, upon his dismal roll;
And where the uncle, and the aunt, was laid
Th' unconscious sheep reposed upon the blade:
And there the village children came to play
To while the intervals of school away.
Whilst recent mourners, from a distance come,
Pass slowly onwards to the silent tomb: *   *   *
And there the tattlers of the neigh'rhood hie,
Inventing falsehoods for the village cry:
There, country swains and damsels meet and weep,
Or laugh, away the moments prior to sleep,—
Make love,—unthoughtful that the sacred sod,
On which they stand or sit belongs to God!

CHAPTER THE SECOND.

I.

Five moons revolv'd, and one revolving then,
Transported Arnold o'er the refluent main.
At home, and safely housed at Rollingate,
(Install'd dictator of his own estate,)
He plann'd the journey to that sylvan bow'r
Where stood the cot, and urg'd his anxious tour:
Consider'd well the steps that he should take;
And how t' approach the little shingle-gate,

O'er-arch'd with honeysuckle in full bloom,
Which form'd the portal to that humble home.
Forth Arnold went: he listen'd, heard the clock—
The only sound within, then gave a knock:
He knock'd again: remained in deep suspense:
Went round the oak, on to the rearward fence:
There he beheld, with his unerring eye,
Jane Hollybrand! he spoke: thus her reply :—
" My father is at work, sir, in the field
Preparing there the fallow to be till'd;
And, sir, I'm sure he never will consent
For me to leave this humble tenement,—
Nay: all the promises on earth will not
Suffice t' induce him let me leave this cot:"
(Now all the time this conversation pass'd
Persuasive Arnold's hand in Jane's was clasp'd;
But she could not, so timid, understand
Wherefore and why he thus desired her hand.)
" And, sir, my mother has been long since dead,
And father, only, earns our daily bread:"
Continued Jane: "but if you'd like to go
To see my father, where you observe the plough,*
And you should find him willing to comply,
Why sir,"   *   *   *   She paus'd, and wept, a tear fell
        from her eye !—
Her heart was full: and, blushing, fain would cry.

---

* Pointing to the field, which could be seen from the garden, where they
were standing.

II.

Now Arnold saw, and ventur'd the first kiss !
And said (the while her hand still lock'd in his)
" You do not know me, do you?—O ! sweet girl.
Ope those bright eyes, and turn aside that curl.
And try if you can recollect in me
The one who kiss'd and vow'd he lovèd thee
Full fifteen years ago. Come," Arnold said.
(Thus as he spoke Jane gently rais'd her head)
" Come, dearest maiden, pray thee be not shy
Believe the truth, believe me ; nay : I'll die
Rather than I'll deceive thee." Then Jane sigh'd.
Desired to speak and lean'd against his side.
    To his request she answer'd modestly :—
" Through yonder gateway, thence by yonder tree,
Pass through the little furze-brake, o'er the bridge,
Turn to your right—along the violet hedge,
And there I trust you'll find him, sir." So he
Fail'd not t' obey th' instructions cheerily.
George saw him coming o'er the fallow ground ;
Hail'd to the horses ; paus'd, and turn'd around,
And bow'd obedience. " Ah ! good Hollybrand,"
Said Arnold, (whilst embracing George's hand,*)
" I seek thy daughter, and I trust t' obtain
Thy sanction, George, to marry dearest Jane,
Some future day when matters are arrang'd."
This sudden salutation quickly chang'd
The countenance of George : he stood amaz'd :
Held down his head and on the fallow gaz'd.

* And familiarising with him, preliminary to the question.

(No doubt poor Hollybrand, as he appear'd,
Was much confounded; and perhaps he fear'd
More sorrows were in store for him : but no !
For Heaven was smiling on his honest brow.)
Then, in reply, with falt'ring accents spoke :
" I fear, dear sir, thou meanest but a joke."
" Nay, nay," the suitor said, and thus : " I find,
Dear Hollybrand, none other to my mind ;
And should you condescend to give to me
Thy daughter's hand, thou shalt survey
My flocks and herds, and guide my husbandry.
Rememb'rest thou, good Hollybrand, the day—
At least you must have heard your daughter say—
When I, to bid my uncle to the hall,
Came in all haste—as aunt had had a fall—
Unto thy cot ?—'t was then I first espied
Thy dearest child ; altho' she vainly tried
T' escape my observation : and when you   *   *   *"
George Hollybrand look'd up ! believ'd it true :
" I do remember well," he said, " the deed you name
And in thy countenance discern the same.—
The Prews (said George) are now, alas ! no more,—
Her* haughty spirit's levell'd with the poor ;
But he, the squire, so bountiful and good,
Will ne'er be equall'd in this neighbourhood ;
In him a father, I may say, I found :
As to the menial friendly to the hound :
He lov'd my child, and when the good man died
As for a father so poor Janie cried.
But, sir, the step which you propose to take

* The deceased Lady Prew.

Is one, I'm sure for my dear daughter's sake,
Requires consideration ; and 't is fraught
With desolation to my little cot."
While George thus said,—Lord Arnold, deep in
      thought,
Conceived * * * and urg'd * * * to which
      George gave consent ;
Released the plough, and to the cottage went.
Meanwhile, observant, Jane had busy been,
Had sought her toilet, and withdrew a " queen ; "
(Whilst lordly Jove had 'woke the latent fire,
And junior Cupid fann'd her meek desire ;)
Thus she appear'd, tho' plain was her attire.

III.

When now the oak had split in countless streams
The mid-day monarch's bright propitious beams,—
A branch of which reflected through the door*
Spread, transiently, a carpet o'er the floor,—
Jane sat expectant, watch'd with anxious care
The mutual movements of th' approaching pair :
At length their voices fell upon her ear,
And she retards a half-unconscious tear,
Withdraws in haste into the inner room ;
There speculates upon her likely doom—
Until she hears the gate's familiar sound,—
And hence their footsteps on the pebbled ground.
They enter.   Now, her father bids her come
And welcome Arnold to their hallow'd home :

* The doorway.

His kindly voice she instantly obeys,
Thus sheds the lustre of her beaming eyes.
Renewing his embraces, Arnold strove
To comfort and console her with his love ;
And re-assured her, with a winning smile,
That in his breast there lurk'd no inward guile :
The tone and accent of his gentle voice
Made honest Hollybrand, for once, rejoice ;
Who, long inured to oft-recurring grief—
As oft to Heaven consign'd his pray'rful brief—
Now, as his wont, he trusted, found relief.

IV.

Then Jane, obedient to her father's will,
Brought forth a pitcher of their household ale,
And from the larder at the cottage rear
The frugal remnant of a well-fed steer,—
With which, and some brown-bread, she form'd a feast,
To entertain—as best they could—their noble guest :
And not untimely was the feast supplied,
Partook, digested, and right-well enjoy'd.
    The amber goblet pass'd from hand to hand,
And as it pass'd—a health to Hollybrand,
Else his dear daughter Jane, with good intent ;
They in return return'd the compliment :
So pass'd the meal.   Now, to confirm his vow,
The earnest suitor kiss'd Jane's virtuous brow ;
Reveal'd a compact, and then read it o'er ;
And, pointing to the impression which it bore,
Said, " There, dear Hollybrand, and Jane, you see
My signature is set, in all sincerity :

With thee I'll leave it, and my honour too,
As the best pledge of my designs to you ;—
Take it," said Arnold, " as my heart—my whole—
For it contains the promptings of my soul :
May God bear witness to the solemn deed !
And now I ask, dear George, are you agreed ?"
The emphasis with which these words were spoke'
(Whilst modest Hollybrand the paper took)
Produced a meet sensation !—hence a pause
Consistent with th' importance of the cause.
Then George into the inner room withdrew
To scan the documents, in earnest, through :
He saw : believ'd the signature was real,
And also recognis'd the ancient seal.

V.

Strange it might seem—that George, this afternoon,
Should recollect—'though thirteen years had flown—
He had, secreted, at his own command
A ready answer to the lord's demand,—
Yet so it was ; and where the secret lay
He interposed and brought it prone to day :
Thus thought the man : and now unto his eyes
An artificial medium he applies,—
Compares the image* which should be the test,
And which would rob or give his temples rest :
" Ah ! (he exclaim'd) it is, it is the same ;"
And having thus discern'd his honor'd name,

---

* A portion of a letter, which bore the impression of the seal of the late
Lord Mountjoy, and which old Squire Prew had ;on the occasion of one of
his visits; left at the cottage.

Return'd with joy and, smiling, said " Dear Sir,
Thou art the late Lord Mountjoy's son 'tis clear :
And now, (said Hollybrand, whilst in the act
Of holding forth and pointing to the fact)
This truth unquestionably doth impel
The answer I now give : God speed thee well—
O Arnold, friend indeed !" (with scarce control
O'er the emotions of his manly soul.)—
And thus—with falt'ring speech, and quite unnerv'd,
" I give my bond, for thou hast well deserv'd
My dearest child, for thy integrity—
Thy gentleness—and generosity."
" Well, Hollybrand, I'm glad your mind 's at ease,"
Said Arnold Mountjoy, " for thy daughter's is ;—
In thy brief absence she has thrice confess'd
The silent promptings of her youthful breast :
Henceforth our lives must interwoven be,
And this the dawn of thy prosperity."
    (Now the adventure, thus concisely told ;
Nor less concise and pleasant, as so bold ;
Provided—that within a month, or two,
The " cottage queen " should with her lover go
To Rollingate ; and there, God willing it,
Domesticated at his noble seat,
She should be educated, and prepare
To share the duties of the " lordly heir."
Till then Lord Arnold thought it ill-advis'd
The marriage contract should be solemniz'd ;—
" I've friends," said he, " who then I must invite—
Whose presence our good manners must requite :"
And twelve months hence he felt convinc'd dear Jane
Would those accomplishments of life attain :

Twelve other months, besides, George then shall see
His virgin daughter at the altar, free—
Free as the zephyrs which combine the air,—
For he had sworn he'd never trespass there,
Or jeopardize her sovereign right to be
The wife of him who wins her lawfully.)
    To this,* like as a harp without the hand,
Stood speechless unpretending Hollybrand ;
And, waiting 'til the impulse bade him speak,
Diverts a tear from his imbrownèd cheek ;
Then he, in language not inapt, begun :
" Thy father, Arnold, must have loved his son !"—
But as his heart had urged him thus to say
His tongue grew pow'rless and refused t' obey.

VI.

The sun was sinking in the far-off west ;
The hour was near at hand for labourers' rest ;
And the fair moon, ascending to invest
The vast impurpling dome of coming night
With her transcendent beams of silvery light,
Was riding onward in her chair of state ;
While he†—her lord and sovereign potentate—
Roll'd down th' horizon o'er the western seas
To render day to the Antipodes.
Dear Philomela, issuing from its cave,
Peal'd forth its plaint upon the breezy wave ;
And whilst gratuitous its hymn, thus given,
Was floating on the balmy winds of heaven—

---

* The preceding sentence—" And this the dawn of thy prosperity."
† The Sun.

Arnold embraced the moments as they flew,
Kiss'd his dear girl, prepared for his adieu,
And bade farewell,—but ere the last was spoken
He'd made a promise never to be broken;
('Less Death, regardless of the night, the day,
Should interpose his awful majesty ;)
And to impress with due solemnity
The parting vow on these meek peasantry
He gave to Jane—himself proud of the gift—
A locket which his grandmother had left
Him when a babe, which (dazzling to the eyes,
Of envious worth and of capacious size,)
" You'll keep," he said, "until I have fulfill'd
The bond which now is in thy breast instill'd :
And you, dear Hollybrand, pray deign t' receive
Before from thy dear cot I take my leave
This little token* of my kind regards—
'T will tell thee, George," said Arnold, " more than
        words—
Far more than I at this late hour can tell :"
And with these gifts he bade them both farewell !
    Whilst Arnold Mountjoy to the village trod ;
The cottagers confided in their God.

VII.

Then night.   Then day : and blithesome chanticleer
Imposed his matin on the sleepers' ear.
    As forth resplendent Sol inflames the sky
In wakeful mood the village freemen hie,—

* A purse containing some gold.

Some with the scythe inflict the sun-brown'd blade,
Whilst some,* unworthy, 'sue their idle trade;
But those upholders of th' industrial arm
Shall be at peace when idlers feel alarm :
The first, their features tell the healthiest tale,
While they, the last, are dirty, thin, and pale :
Along the lanes the perfumes as they rise
The former greet, the latter would despise.
Go ! slothful saunt'rer on the road of life
And earn thy bread—return unto thy wife,
(It may be children, too, thou hast at home—
If home thou hast—who wait their usual doom,)
With smiling countenance ; and doff the cry
Offensive t' th' ear, and spurn such charity,
And leave the generous alms to sick and poor—
Whose age or frailty, man ! deserves them more.

VIII.

The while the day the villagers improve,
Lord Arnold Mountjoy 's briskly on the move
On the main road to Rollingate, and fain
"Old John," the coachman, renders up the rein.
Now, as his wont, where'er the coach delays,
At measured stages for the meet relays,
Regales "old John ;" (whose rough refulgent nose—
The fruits, apparent, of an over-dose—
Seems more protub'rant as he onward goes :)
With studied complaisance and kindly word
Drinks health and happiness to his fair lord ;

* Vagrant beggars.

Indulges in an extra glass, or two,
In honor of his lordship ; whom he knew
To be "a whip" most excellently true.
    About this period* some folks talk'd of steam's
Surpassing everything in shape of teams :
In northern counties railroads were being made,
Which had a tendency to mar John's trade,—
And nothing more provoking could be said,
Or cast more horror in the poor man's head :
"Give me," said he, "my dear old four-in-hand,
And twelve relays, I'll drive throughout the land—
From 'John O'Groat's' down to the Cornish coast,—
(Now this, of course, was rather a bit of boast)
Tell me," he said, "can steam come up to this?"
To answer strongly would have been amiss ;
So those who knew the circle of his brain
Permitted him his fancy to retain—
Expounding his ideas with much force,
Whilst Arnold whistled† to the leading horse
And in due time came up to his lodge-gate,—
The gothic entrance into Rollingate ;
Resign'd the whip to John's triumphant care,
And gave a "blessing‡" o'er the usual fare :
"Thank ye, my lord :" (repeated John, and loud)—
And thus : "Good bye, yer honor," then, more proud
Than e'er, resumes his place, commands the steed ;
Th' entangled whip dis'tangled and then freed
Forth in the air assumes th' impressive scream :

---

* The early part of the nineteenth century, the date when the incidents
which form this poem are to be considered to have their origin.
    † Whistling of the whip.
    ‡ Something over the proper fare.

" Now talk to me, if you like, about your steam !—
It 's all a myth : God knows it 's all a dream."
Th' obsequious horses, anxious for their part,
Reply to John's " kic-kic," and off they start.

IX.

Now of the journey : one can well conceive
The numerous incidents which tend t' relieve
The dull monotony of such a tour,
And thus make sweet the elsewise tedious hour,
That constant friend,* prince of the upper main,
Was scarce molested† from the rosy dawn
Until he rounded o'er the distant hills—
When there forth swung (as he revolving swells)
Promiscuous clouds across his fiery way
And spread, like beacon-fires, the closing day.
    Thus advantageous 'neath umbrageous trees,
Which rustled in the June-time fragrant breeze,
Th' aspiring peasantry as blithe as gay
Enjoy the intervals of making hay,—
Round went the tea, or round the home-brew'd ale,
And thus they transiently themselves regale ;
And now and then, as each in turn doth quaff
The timely cup, uproarious 'rose a laugh.
    A drover now, with breast bare to the sun,
Inquired the hour, and urg'd the cattle on ;
His ashen beam fell sore upon their loins,
And with the lash some imprecation joins ;
They, in reply to the unrighteous law,

* The sun.   † Obscured.

Reluctantly obey the fellsome blow.

Again : some practised beggars plead for alms
In moanful accent, and with dirty palms ;
Some kindly creature on the coach throws down
A copper coin or two ; they smile or frown,
According as the gift is small or great,
And then again they lazily retreat,—
Repeating, most persistently, the cry
To whomsoever may be passing by :
Perhaps at night, some place offensive slunk,
They curse the giver and get beastly drunk.

And then th' eccentric roadside "public" signs,*
Grotesquely figured, and inscribed with lines
As various writ as various the designs :—
"The Rose and Crown." "The Stag." "The Bull."
    "The Bear."
The "Coach and Horses." "Horses, Hounds, and
    Hare."
"The Rising Sun." "The Seven Stars." "Half-
    moon."
"The Maid and Magpie:" and "The Old Green
    Man."
Of "Heads"—The Duke's: The Queen's: The King's.
    "King's Arms."—
High-colour'd frontages, whose wondrous charms—
To the unwary—oft are fraught with ill ;
While he, the "landlord," dotes upon his till.
All these† attend to make the trav'ler smile,
To less' the length, as 't were, of every mile.

---

* Public-house signboards.
† The various incidents recorded in this section.

X.

When Arnold reach'd his own paternal hall,
(As punctual to his word as the great ball
Which in the morn fulfils the promis'd boon,
Or as, at night, comes forth the gracious moon,
By God's consent,) he took his pen and wrote
With dexterous hand the first momentous note ;
For otherwise the moment would be lost
To catch, at the lodge-gate, the evening post :
'Tis done : and now along the turnpike main
The mail bears on the destiny of Jane.

XI.

Next, when this first and most propitious brief
Had reach'd the cot, alternate joy and grief
With equal pressure influenc'd Jane's breast,
And oft at night prevented needful rest ;
Her sire, (as she,) alternately would sigh,—
As oft he smil'd as oft bedew'd his eye :
" A month," said George, " will soon have pass'd
        away,
And then a week, and then another day,
And then the moment when my child is gone !—
And I (he said most sorrowf'lly), alone !"
Jane sobb'd and sigh'd, whilst George desired her
        cease—
" It 's all for good, my dear, come be at peace,"
Said he ; but no,—her heart, poor girl, was full :
No human solacy could then control

Her virtuous bosom ; nought could check the flood,
Until she clasp'd her hands and look'd to God !
And then she scann'd the cottage whitewash'd walls,
Where hung a picture of " Niag'ra Falls ;"
'Mong several others—one, our Saviour's birth,*
Seem'd, of them all, the one of greatest worth,
For she had learnt to love Him : then again
Jane read the letter in more hopeful strain,
And grew more reconciled unto her fate :
Some of her childhood scenes she'd 'numerate ;—
To Jane's sweet memory would oft recur
The fun and frolic at the village fair,—
Held once a year,—and whither she would go
To hear the bumpkin band, and see the " show :"
This was a happy period of her life :
Her mother liv'd, and was a loving wife
To Hollybrand.　(Ah ! George had praised her so
That when she died most dreadful was the blow.)†
　As then each Sunday morning came along
Jane heard the village-church bells go ding-dong,
(When her dear mother liv'd and stay'd at home)
And, with her father, forth would early roam
To pay their homage on the Sabbath day,
In God's own house.　The villagers would say
(Though with a sort of semi-jealous air)—
" That Jenny gain'd admirers everywhere :"
Well ! no one, rich or poor, could pass her by
Without being charm'd with her impressive eye :

---

* The proper title of this picture was, no doubt, " The birth of our
Saviour."
　† Afiliction.

And whilst at church she rais'd her voice to God,
Was never seen to chatter, laugh, or nod :
And never fail'd to gather every word,
As it would fall upon her list'ning ear :—
Sometimes poor "Jenny" dropp'd a silent tear,
And some kind folks began to pity her—
Poor girl ; for then her mother lay so ill,
It almost made the child, herself, unwell.
T' her poor dear mother she'd read the Sunday book,
Turn up her eyes and with a solemn look—
Yet with a kind of smile—say this (and more)—
"O Lord, have mercy on the sick, and poor !"

XII.

Jane now began (as Arnold wish'd) to arrange
Her little wardrobe, for th' approaching change.
From humble life she soon was to withdraw
To Rollingate,—there learn the " genteel law,"
'Midst scenes of gaiety ; (but yet aloof ;)—
To learn in private, 'neath the mansion roof,
The necessary etiquette—for she
The future hope of Arnold was to be.
  Tears flow'd, and oft, as day and night flew past ;
More often still at every eve-repast :
The cottage-home serenity had fled ;
And George look'd forward with an earthly dread
To that sad day ; his very heart recoil'd—
To think of parting with his only child !
But Hollybrand, though passionately fond,
  Had giv'n his word, and hence fulfill'd his bond.

XIII.

At length the month, the week, the day had flown,
And high in heav'n revolved the silent moon,—
The night had come ; and (save the poor girl's heart,
Which now began to fail and dread to part)
All's ready : but the evening's pensive shade
Unmann'd the heart, o'er forty years had made :
Poor George felt sad—indeed, well, well he might—
Whilst pondering o'er the last long-dreaded night ;
He knew too well that when the morning came
To him his child would only be a name.
Thus then to pray'rs :—Upon their bended knee
They sent their orisons forth unto God, that He
Would grant to them (especially to her)
His favoring spirit, and His bounteous care.
And from its bounds the briny-liquid lept,
For Hollybrand could not refrain, and wept :
The last "good night," with intermissive sighs,
Fell from their lips ; while 'kerchiefs to their eyes
Detain'd their tears :   Such was the dreary eve
Of that lone day when " Jenny" took her leave.

XIV.

Red 'rose the sun, and flush'd the fleecy sky ;
His 'fulgent rays foretold the hour was nigh
When soon the cottagers would ope their eye,
For chanticleer had loos'd his horny bill,
And sent abroad his unmistaken thrill.
That honor'd oak bore up a motley throng

Of feathery warblers, lively with their song ;
Beneath the tree the chickens 'wait the hour,
Then rush like steeple-chasers to the door :
And, helter-skelter, forth the bristled beast
With usual manners begg'd their usual feast :
(Could they have known their mistress sigh'd and
    cried,
No doubt the cloven group would have denied
Themselves one meal at least; and would have
    mourn'd
With Hollybrand, his loss ; for Jane adorn'd
That little cot so long, 't was sure unkind
To leave it now, and everything behind :)
But Jane came not, as usual, forth to feed
The drowsy grunters ; so, to lull their greed,
George did for once (but not without much pain)
Strew out, among them all, the crumbs and grain,
And fill'd the trough.   'T was now the hour of eight,
When lo ! they heard a noise,—the birds took flight, ---
'T was like the sound of carriages afar :
At length they see the fastly-driven car.
Jane then, 'mid hopes and fears, tripp'd 'cross the floor
And saw the coach advancing to the door !
Another moment, whilst, embracing her,
Lord Arnold's kisses stayed the falling tear.
His mode of greeting, and his gentle grace,
Implanted joy-looks on poor George's face ;—
For Arnold's winning manners never fail'd
To cheer the hearts of those whom grief assail'd :
    They all sit down (the morning meal is spread),
But George, at times, seem'd sad and sore afraid ;
At intervals he scarcely could restrain

N

From weeping: Arnold now announc'd to Jane
The time was fast approaching when, in fact,
Her luggage in the carriage should be pack'd :
Then she, in answer, to her room repairs
And, more serene, her humble self prepares ;
Return'd, and what ? a picture to behold,—
Her eyes like diamonds unadorn'd with gold :
With hasty steps she gain'd her father's side ;
Her lifted hands a screen became, to hide
Once more her sad and saturated cheek :
In tones subdued, unnerv'd, she tries to speak,
(Her words were 'sunder'd with repeated sighs,)
And then a pause ; and then again she tries,
Say'ng—" Father, father, oh ! 't is sad to part ;
But, father, trust in God, and cheer your heart."
These were the words, the parting words of those
Whose cottage sanctity was just about to close.
One moment more must bring that last " farewell,"—
Whose import—none but George and Jane could tell ;
And Hollybrand, now left alone to dwell !

XV.

George, recollecting Arnold's solemn vow,
Bethought himself of future joy : and so—
In silent solitude—he work'd away,
And tried to gather comfort through the day.
He doubted not that Arnold would redeem
The solemn pledges he had made to him—
That he should come and live on his estate,—
Live at the lodge and keep the entrance-gate :

(Adjoining which were well-plann'd premises,
For cows or pigs ; for chickens, ducks or geese :)
And there, such things should be at his command,
As compensation for his daughter's hand :
This, for his life-time, should be set apart ;
Together with a nice light horse-and-cart.
But ere this possibly could be enjoy'd,
Full eight months more, his time must be employ'd
At Westonbury,—there (in sun or shade)
To serve the year's engagement he had made
With the new occupants now at the Hall ;—
For all the Prews were gone—yes, one and all
Were gone to their long home ! So George worked on
Until these eight months' solitude had flown :
But not a week pass'd by without the post
Convey'd to Hollybrand (from one who cost
Him many a tear) a letter ; which scann'd o'er,
Infused in George—a hundred times or more—
A gleam of joy ; and, oft when he would pore
Each well-filled page, he'd turn to her dear name,
Imprint a kiss—and then infold the same.

CHAPTER THE THIRD.

I.

Now (retrospective of the hour of sighs—
Disconsolate moments—inundated eyes),
When disconcerted George look'd, but in vain !
As Arnold bore away his daughter Jane,

The trundled dust uprising points the way,
But disappoints his all-observant eye ;
Obedient then to its instructive mood
His heart, relaxing, propagates the flood.
      The Great All-ruler of a cloudless sky
Roll'd on and on the lovely lamp of joy,
And shed its holiness o'er nature's face ;
And thus, Omniscient, with compelling grace,
Ordain'd the products of the bounteous earth,
All in due season, to come smiling forth.
      (Such was the hour and such the transient day
When Arnold's carriage roll'd along the way.)
Ah !   Who the Artist,—Whose the skilful hand
Impels the beams which fructify the land?
'Tis He, 'tis His, who governs earth and air,
Who pois'd the sun, the moon, and every star,
And who directs them morning, noon, and night,
Yea, ever since He said : and gave the light !
      The painter imitates with studied stroke
The ruffled ocean, or the stirring brook ;
But where the roarings of the troubled main
So well defined upon the painted plain ?
Or where's the music of the humble thrush,
So well depicted by his able brush
Perch'd on yon twig of nut-brown hazel-bush ?
Or where the whisperings of the rustling trees,
As through their branches curl the gentle breeze ?—
Or, when 'presented in a wintry storm,
We hear no moaning through the leafless form.
      And then again—behold his* emerald glade

---

* The painter's.

How breezy-bent it greets the crescent blade,
When, as it were, ten mowers (rosy blithe)
Advance by steps and sway the merc'less scythe ;
Aye : how so natural the golden grain
Seems, aged-like, incline to earth again,
And, as the harvesters with rigid eye
Thrust forth the sickle most contemptuously,
How great the fall ; but where the weapon's cry ? * * *

II.

While thus the muse compares the works of God
With that of man, twelve miles of country road
Had borne the pressure of the chariot-wheel,
Since George and Jane partook their parting meal.
And here—a quaint secluded neighbourhood—
Just where the ruins of a convent stood,
A group of gipsies (tented in a cove)
Bore tokens of contentment and of love :
One of the tribe advanced towards the coach,
And begg'd permission that she might approach :
Lord Arnold stopp'd, and lent his gen'rous ear,
Whilst she address'd him with a gentle air :
And then, observing Arnold's willing smile,
(He not unmindful of their practis'd guile)
Rehears'd a story with considerable tact,
And hard-endeavoured to enforce the fact—
Peace and prosperity for thee 's in store,
For thou art generous to the sick and poor !
" 'Two years from now," she said, " thou shalt repair
To Hymen's altar with your lady-fair ;
And when, dear sir, the nuptial hour shall come

Much joy shall reign at thy paternal home :
Then, when twelve moons their course hath duly run,
Thy virtuous wife shall bless thee with a son :"
This startling prophecy astounded Jane,
Who seem'd desirous to proceed again ;
But ere they started Arnold threw her down
A goodly portion of a " half-a-crown :"
" God bless you sir," she pleasingly replies :
" And you, dear lady, with those lucky eyes,—
Ten thousand comforts 'wait thee in thy bow'r ;
And Heav'n shall smile upon thy wedding-hour."
Then Arnold, gathering in the careless rein,
Inclined his whip across the horses' mane ;
They bend their twin-like necks as they proceed,
And soon attain the regulated speed.
 The converse now continued for awhile
Upon the subject of the gipsy's tale ;
When Jane, consistent with her lowly sphere,
Relieved her eye of an incredulous tear :
Her hope was where it had continually soar'd,
And forth in secret there her pray'rs were pour'd.
E'en, as the coach resum'd the onward course,
A thought struck Arnold, with emphatic force,—
That this sly woman, dexterous and sedate,
Might have inform'd herself on the estate :
" How cunning," thought he ; " well, it is their trade,
And fools are often innocently made."

III.

As day wore on—the evening-hour of eight
Brought them within a league of Rollingate :

There the old house stood in a pleasant vale,
'Mid goodly elms and oaks which stem the gale,
And which commandingly arose to view ;
The pale-blue smoke curl'd up anon anew ;
And on a mound the flag-staff bore on high
The family-banner, in the sun-set sky.
Above—there waited the pale queen of night,
With her retaining beams of holy light ;
Then condescending to the happy pair—
When Sol had vanish'd—strew'd her silvery care :
O righteous moon, refulgent in the skies !—
All poets greet thee with their longing eyes ;—
Thou art to them a river of delight ;
Their choicest pages praise thee with their might :
Unnumber'd titles to thy form are given,
As they behold thee in th' unbounded heaven :
Soul-stirring Byron loved the night, and strove
T' immortalise thee as " the lamp of love."
(Another tries thy title to improve.)
Most welcome were its hallow'd beams to those
Whose long day's journey drew near to a close.
    Th' exhausted horses knew the well-trod ground,
And long'd to hear the groom's inducing sound ;
The grooms, they listen, and are glad to hear
The distant rumbling which disturbs the deer :
The whizzing whip re-echoed through the trees,
And Arnold's voice came with the western breeze,—
The sound increased as forth they onward bore
In steady paces, to the mansion-door.
    High up, in night, now sat " The dark-robed
        moon ;"*

* See Ossian's " Songs of Selma."

Whilst round about her purple-drapèd throne,
The assembled twinklers—brilliantly array'd—
Unite in love to welcome forth the maid.
Great is the joy throughout the boundless vast.
Imagination sent a silvery blast
To 'wake the nightingales ; the birds uprise
And pour their melodies into the skies.

The inmates of the mansion, hast'ning forth,
Beheld (they said) an angel come on earth ;—
No greater beauty, say they, could exist
Than she, on whom their eyes were firmly fixt :
When through the hall Jane, trembling, passèd by
They saw, unveil'd, her brilliant sparkling eye
As round she gazed upon the chandeliers,
That here and there lit up the winding stairs ;
And swords and bucklers, which had hung for years,
Seem'd coalescing, with the central vase*
Which saved its perfumes until then, and rose
In all its fresh and lovely fragrancy
To greet the stranger : but, Lord Arnold, he
Observing his dear Jane's timidity
Hail'd Toogood,† who (both elderly and kind,
And one to whom Jane could unfold her mind)
Came 'cross the hall, and bow'd and shook the hand
And made th' acquaintance of Jane Hollybrand.

* Of flowers.
† An elderly aunt, formerly a faithful companion to the late Lady Mountjoy.

IV.

Transcendent morn 'rose o'er yon barley-field ;
But dusky clouds fly'ng 'cross the golden shield
Dispersed his beams ; yet, he controll'd the main,
And usher'd in a brighter day for Jane.
   She 'wakes (her wonted hour), looks 'round and
      finds
Rich damask drapery for her window-blinds !
Chairs, almost fairy-like with 'lastic touch,
Resemble the impurpled-cover'd couch.
Then half-recumbent lo : the gentle girl
Beholds the furniture inlaid with pearl !
Herself she now reflectedly espies,
But scarce believing her yet slumb'rous eyes—
'Til, opportune, the wardrobe glass disclosed
The doubtful myst'ry ; then she grew composed,
Alighted venturously on the soft floor,
And scann'd the toilet o'er and o'er and o'er :
She timorously removes* the window-blind ;
Observes, with pleasure, the fantastic hind,
The antler'd buck, the mother and her fawn ;
And all the beauties of the verdured lawn.
The ivy tendrils kiss'd her window-pane,
And further rearward wound the jessamine
With other fragrant vines.   Now, Jane, she makes
Another survey t'wards the glist'ning lakes :
There she beholds, most gracefully afloat—
The silvery swans ; and there the anchor'd boat
Hugg'd the green bank.   All nature smiles, as 't were ;

---

* Drawing aside.

And passing showèrs cool'd the atmosphere:
While birds among* made music sweet and clear.
  On bended knee, Jane's orisons had flown
With the appearance of the saffron dawn :
So now (rememb'ring Arnold's fond desire
To breakfast with her), in her best attire,
She decks herself—expectant of a knock :
Mid joy and grief she hears the tuneful† clock,
Which crown'd the summit of the mansion mews,—
The time arrived : now Jane once more re-views
Her humble self, and modestly prepares * * *
When lo !—she hears a patting on the stairs,
And hies obediently across the floor—
To welcome Toogood at the appointed hour :
With all the sweetness of her youth, she said—
" Oh dear ! dear ma'am (and sigh'd) I really dread
To leave the room ;" but when Aunt Toogood smil'd
And bade Jane cheer, thus say'ng : " Come, come, my
        child
(In such a winsome mood) and follow me,
For Arnold now is anxious, 'waiting thee,"
She doff'd her trepidness, and went the way.
And so began the duties‡ of the day.

v.

All now goes well : the breakfast-meal is o'er :
Her Arnold takes her for a morning-tour,
Points out the beauties of the oak and elm,
And other grandeurs of his little realm ;

---

* The branches.   † The chimes.   ‡ Family prayers.

Then guides her to th' embankment of the lake—
Where various water-fowl their jauntings take,
And make—in common with their kindred race—
Untarnish'd pleasure and conjugal peace :
With some persuasion Arnold gain'd consent,
Releas'd the boat ; then on the lake is spent
A pleasant cruise, 'til sundry drops of rain
Fell lustily and ringleted the main.
Each fleet intruder from the upper air
Involves the cruisers in increasing care ;
The skiff 's made fast, and both with speed return
Along a route through laurel, myrtle, fern ;
Soon as they gain the lofty portico
Down pours the rain,—a thousand riv'lets flow.
 When, as the clouds have broke, th' incumbent
  drops—
Like diamonds strewn about the verdant crops—
Sway to and fro in answer to the breeze,—
The bending blade directs them by degrees
Down to the mould ; thus mingled with the roots
The earth brings forth its seasonable fruits,
And nature laughs. How good such transient
 showers,
Unguentous to the parched herbs and flowers !—
The shrubs are cleans'd, as though re-varnish'd o'er,
And Horus now shines out with greater pow'r.

VI.

Ascendant in the heav'ns the monarch reigns.
 Noon (all-defiant in th' imperial plains),
Surnamed Meridian, bends his mystic bow,

And waits the assault of his presumptuous foe ;*
But grew despairingly as forth he came
(Like heav'n and earth combin'd in one great flame.)
Towards the vertex of the brazen arch.
But as he came, and with prodigious march,
Meridian waver'd, and declined the fray :
Thus onward Horus roll'd triumphantly !
The god, though angry with this vain pretence,
Forgave Meridian the unjust offence,—
On this condition—that he† 'd ne'er again
Dispute his passage through the vaulted main.
Meridian thankfully received the boon,
And thus renounced all title to the throne.

VII.

Just as Meridian felt so dire dismay'd,
And ever after so discomforted,
The luncheon-bell invited forth the guest—
To be partakers of the mid-day feast :
Such food and drinkables meet for the hour
Were attributes most welcome, since the tour
Occasion'd such exertion to obtain
The much desired shelter from the rain :
Thus then refresh'd, retiring to her room
Jane penn'd her first epistle to th' old home ;
(Ah me ! how sweet " th' old home " falls on the ear
To all to whomsoever " home " is dear.)
In language of simplicity she wrote
Thus : (now in strictest confidence we quote)—

---

* The Sun.   † Meridian.

" My dearest father.   We arriv'd last night
At Rollingate (thank gracious God) all right ;
We halted twice, refresh'd ourselves, drove on,—
Most truly thankful when the day was done :
Before I laid me down I bent my knee
And pray'd to Him above to comfort thee ;
Arose this morning, breakfasted, and talk'd,
Then 'round the grounds we comfortably walk'd ;
We rowed upon the lake among the swans,
And fell in love with all the little ones ;
Just then a rapid show'r began to fall,
We hasten'd back and luncheon'd in the Hall :
All now is quiet ; Arnold 's very kind
And I, dear father, happier in mind.
     That dear old lady, whom you heard him say
Was such a motherly creature, said to-day
That all at Rollingate were proud of me ;
So now, dear father, pray thee happy be :
Next week, I purpose, you shall hear again.
     Believe me   *   *   *   yours affectionately, Jane."
Then came the thoughts of how she should proceed
To get it posted, and the postage freed,
But just that instant Toogood happily came,
And Jane's distress dissolv'd into a name :
The compliant footman took it to the lodge,
And there consigned it to old Andrew Hodge.
     "Old Andrew," now, was seventy years of age ;
(Had come to Rollingate erst as a page ;)
O'er fifty years, it was the old man's boast,
He had been guardian of th' important post :
But then, besides, he rode about th' estate,—
A sort of bailiff over Rollingate,

And superintendent of the flocks and herds,
The deer, the swine, and the domestic birds,—
He made arrangements for the annual sale
Of surplus cattle ; oak, and ashen, pale ;
The over-crowding firs and elms and pines ;
And kept with strict regard the bound'ry lines ;
Such then was Andrew's alternating work,
With his kind niece at home as medium clerk.
Though now the poor old man had grown infirm
From partial palsy in his dexter* arm,
And sometimes suffer'd almost martyrdom
With the lumbago in his back and loins,
And painful visitations in his groins ;
So that a few years more like this, distress'd,
Must of necessity send him to rest.

VIII.

In the meantime that dear old Christian dame,
(The bearer of that most appropriate name†—
Who never turn'd a beggar from the door
Without a penny and some surplus store,)
Appriz'd dear Jane that dinner-time was near—
If she would be so kind as to prepare ;
And waited 'til she wash'd and plann'd her hair ;
Whilst Jane made such inquiries which become
So lowly-a stranger to so lordly-a home.
And the blithe bell, diminutive in size,
Sent forth its welcome in the blissful skies —
As though a host of potentates were there

---

* The right arm).   † Toogood.

Prebent on turkey, venison, and hare ;—
Not so just now, yet shall its merry ting
Continue its accustom'd carolling.—
    The time may come again when princely guest
Shall be the bidden-ones unto the feast ;
When round the hall the old ancestral cup
By lords and ladies shall be lifted up ;
But in the interim there is much to do :
Around its orbit twice the world shall go
Before the ancient dignity 's restored,
And knights and squires admixture at the board :
(Yes, two 'volutions round the sun is plann'd
Ere Jane shall doff the name of " Hollybrand,"
For that of " Mountjoy ;" and when that is done
The old festivities shall be begun.)—
    " To-day at dinner there will only be,"
Said Toogood, " Arnold, you—my dear, and me :
But, dearest girl, I have a word to say—
You know that Arnold thinks of going away
A fortnight hence for just a year or two,
For—as he says—the benefit of you,—
Yes, dearest Jane,—the benefit of you !—
He's going, he tells me, to the far-off East—
To Rome, Vienna, Berlin, and Trieste.
In the meantime (please God to grant it so)
Such education as is *apropos*—
For instance : grammar, 'rithmetic, and prose,
Geography, and music, and all those
Embellishments—enrichments of the mind,
And such-like things which make us good and kind,
You'll learn, dear Jane, from gentlemen of wit ;
That with their teaching you may be found fit

To fill the duties which on you will fall
When you are, darling, mistress of the Hall!"
Now this announcement, evidently made
With all affection for the gentle maid
To meliorate the anxiety of mind
Which must accrue, was (doubtless) well design'd;
And equally as well digested, as
Poor Jane, know'ng well how ignorant she was,
Told dear Aunt Toogood of her willingness,
And trusted it would lead to happiness.

IX.

But hark! the festal-bell is ringing loud;
And Toogood, sev'nty-three, as ever proud
Comes strutting through the passage to the hall
In the same silk, and likewise handsome shawl,
That she received at Arnold's christening ball;
Whilst Jane, all in the vigour of her youth,
Leans on her arm—exemplary of truth,
But plainly dress'd; yet with a lovely face;
And paced the passage with a queenly grace.
    Now Arnold meets them and allays alarm—
By his embraces and inviting arm;
Whilst dear Aunt Toogood hastens on before
And blithely deputizes at the door;
Which ceremonial frolicsomely plann'd
Dispell'd those fears that Innocence had fann'd:
Thus then they enter and draw near the board.
    While the vouchsafing grace from God's implored
The savoury viands, which compose the food,
Send up their vapours in consonant mode;

And wines, propitious—in the crystal vase,
Move round in token of th' eventful cause :
The homely meal—as homely as could be
Consistent with Lord Arnold's dignity—
Affords them joy.   Now, while the time beguiles
And peace and plenty, compliments and smiles
Predominate, Lord Arnold of the hour
Avails himself, describes th' intended tour,—
Improving every moment as it flew
With tales fictitious or with stories true ;
Or hum'rously endeavours to explain
The great advantage it will be to Jane,
Whilst he's away ; and what arrangements he
Ordain'd for her improvement and futurity :
His eye beheld her,—fain was he to find
The plan propounded suiting to her mind :
For Jane express'd herself with great delight,
And promised to improve with all her might.

X.

Mark how this hope lit up dear Toogood's breast.—
How her maternal heart seem'd lull'd to rest ;
How she endeavour'd—though 't were vain to try—
To stay the tear now issuing from her eye ;
How she attempted to describe her joy,
And seem'd in raptures with her darling boy !—
At length, as though empower'd by Him on high.
She doffs her tears and draws this imagery—
" There are," she said, " some who make chary wives.
Are blest with families, and live their lives
In sweet contentment, happiness and love,

Whose guardian is the mighty One above ;
But there are others who without a thought
Waste bags of gold and lack at last a groat
Wherewith to pay, and then—but when too late—
In tears discover their impoverish'd state ;
Whilst, on the other hand, those keeping well in
        mind—
Economy, will always comfort find ;
Their homes their castles—whether small or great—
Are ramparts of defence by day or night,—
No bitter whinings, nor remorseless sighs,
Reproachful twitt'rings o'er invented lies,
Are theirs, but truthful love's protectorate :
And may God grant it—so at Rollingate !"—
Such was the purport of Aunt Toogood's tale—
A sort of lecture on a little scale ;
Perhaps experience of some family feud
Had prompted this extemporaneous mood,
Or the remembrance of some ruined pair
Impelled her speech to tell of their despair ;
For 't seemed to give th' old lady much relief
When she had summarised her tale of grief,
As then again her countenance bespoke
Her readiness to embrace a passing joke ;
And she in turn some funny things would say,
Then leave to Jove to solve the mystery ;
Till Night (nocturnal goddess of the skies)
Invades the hall in mystical disguise
And with due courteousness involved their eyes.

XI.

Nine times the earth with its redeeming force
Whirl'd round its vast undeviating course :
Nine times the sun (obscured but only twice)
Obey'd the law and paid his sacrifice :
As oft the moon in reverential robes
Stood forth predominant among the globes ;*
And only once—and that in love it seems—
The halo atmosphere impair'd her beams :
The stars, obedient to the mighty Hand,
Imparted promise to Jane Hollybrand.
But now alas ! alas ! that dreadful pow'r†
Had usher'd in the last and pitiable hour,
When that dissyllable—that dread "farewell"
Will fall from Arnold like a deathful knell !—
But true t' his promise he will faithful be,
Should Heaven preserve him over land and sea,
For love combined with strict integrity
Will well assist him through those trying years,
And turn to joy Jane's first momentous tears.
    When, as reluctantly he turn'd around,
Great Day‡ portray'd him on the gravell'd ground—
Sh' inclined her tearful eyes toward the shade ;
But in the twinkling of an eye it fled :
" Ah me ! (she said) he's gone—yet not for ever ! "
    Now Jane had learnt how painful 't was to sever
From one who dearly lov'd, and whom she lov'd,—
As her demeanour most distinctly prov'd,—
For when she looked (in vain) to see the coach

---

* Stars.   † Time.   ‡ The sun.

Which bore him on, she hurried to her coach
And there * * * but ere she 'd time to vent her grief
Her kind adviser* came to her relief—
" Be cheer'd " she said—and bent to stay Jane's tears,
And solac'd the dear girl with soothing pray'rs :
Then Jane, obedient to th' impulsive move,
Arose and openly confess'd her love.

XII.

The following day, about th' eleventh hour,
Jane heard a "tap-tap" at the parlour door ;
So, suddenly uprising on her feet,
Prepared herself the visitor to meet,—
"The Reverend Alexander Gordon Jay,"†
(Most popular grammar-master of the day, -
Within a circle of near thirty miles,—
A man belov'd by most fair juveniles ;
Of stature small, but of capacious tact ;
And of his person wondrously exact.)—
Who with obeisance and with dexter hand
Proffer'd his friendship to Jane Hollybrand ;
Jane fain reciprocated his intent
And lent herself to the first rudiment ;
Her quick conception of the rule consign'd
Dispell'd the doubts revolving in his mind
So much that he, amaz'd, could not refrain
Adventuring plaudits in becoming strain ;
Thus so far pleased with all that he desired
The doctor bowed and gracefully retired.

* Aunt Toogood.   † D.D.

Thrice weekly, now, Jane's music-master came,—
A Briton, but with an Italian name,—
Who ceremoniously improved the time
With some cadenzas—aiming the sublime—
On one of Broadwood's fine old instruments ;
Then gently introduced his rudiments
(Or some-one-else's) in the key of "C,"
The scale of which Jane master'd dexterously ;
Then, in due time, proceeded on to "G,"
And conquer'd the sharp seventh most famously ;
Engaging now in "sharps" and then in "flats,"—
And all the incidental little thats,*—
In eighteen months she could with moderate ease
Encounter creditably the "Surprise."†

And now, in turn, the dancing-master 'd come,
Release his gloves and make himself "at home ;"
Unsheath his violin, then draw its bow,—
With "this" and "that" and "simply so-and-so,"—
So that he manag'd (medium-way) to please ;
And deem'd, no doubt, he justly earn'd his fees.

At the appointed season of the week,
Her drawing-master, tall and rather sleek,
Veer'd round the back and palm'd the stable-boy ;
Who, quite as willing—for his master's hay
To him cost nothing—fed the craving beast,
Which soon showed symptoms of the welcome feast :
Now Jane ('t is fair to say) did not progress
In this particular art, but nevertheless
She could depict a landscape with such taste
As plainly proved her lessons were not waste.

---

* Appoggiaturas, a musical term.　　† One of Haydn's symphonies.

Thus then, with time and men of such repute
As those engaged for Jane, one could compute
With some degree of certainty and pride
The joys in store for the intended bride.

XIII.

Some weeks had now, thank Providence, pass'd by ;
While swift as coaches, and as ships at sea,
Flew to and fro the sweet epist'lary,
And which convey'd, as dear Aunt Toogood said,
Such faithful vows as lovers love to read ;
For Jane would never fail to read t' her aunt*
The sayings and doings upon the Continent,
Nor fail'd to report minutely and dilate
Those portions which affected Rollingate ;
But always shunn'd the last impressive line
Which bore the language of a Valentine :
This simple act most rigidly observed
Obtain'd for her the credit it deserved.

XIV.

Now Jane, in Arnold's absence, strove and won
Th' affection—nay, the love of every-one—
Of those whose happy lot it was to share
The joys domestic which abounded there,
For all ('t was often said) would run a mile
To catch from her sweet face but half-a-smile ;

---

* She now habitually addressed Mistress Toogood as "Aunt," and not at
all it was thought) improper.

Though smiles were not at all times to be seen
(Alike with peasant, prince, or king, or queen),
For in her loneliness enough would rise
To force a tear-drop from her sparkling eyes ;
At eventide her sorrow seemèd most,
But in her God she never fail'd to trust :
Yes, eventide 's the time when Jane would sigh,
And sometimes—unavoidably—would cry,
As then the thoughts of home would oft recur,
For everything still there to her was dear,—
Ah ! dear—and natural it should be so,—
Could she forget her birth-place?   Oh ! no, no :
Yet something, 'mid her sorrow, whisp'ring, said—
Be calm—be comforted, and not afraid !

XV.

When the blest firmament unruffled is,
And sol's fair consort hastens forth to please ;
When the celestial vault is most serene,
And its ethereal wanderers are seen ;
Such were the moments Jane could best impart
The silent impulse of her tender heart ;
And those the moments that she loved the best—
Preparatory to her going to rest,
For then her orisons ascended high,
And she in peace could close her weary eye.
But when the time came on that Jane could trace
The weeks, the days, the hours, when the blest face
Of her dear father she again would see—
She pass'd her evenings far more pleasantly,
And chatted freely—talk'd about the flowers,

The lovely groves, the avenues, and bowers,
The lakes, and such-like things,—oh, yes ! and then
She'd play, or sing to some p'rhaps favourite strain—
These words—

SONG : TO A STAR.

Sweet blest-born star—for ever winging
  In the chambers of the sky,
Oh ! let me join thee—always singing
  Some enchanting melody.

Yes ! envied beauty, ever busy
  Frisking joys about the air,
Oh ! let me come ere I go crazy—
  Looking, wondering what ye are.

Or if thou wilt not, pray—have pity,
  Carol loud enough that we,
Improving love, may hear thy ditty
  Sung in matchless harmony.

            E. E. F.

XVI.

Now, at the pretty 'lizabethan lodge
There liv'd (as said before) old Andrew Hodge,
Unable to perform on the estate
Aught else—and hardly that—than ope the gate :
No plan more suitable could Jove contrive—
Nor any member of the starry hive—
Than that good George to Rollingate should come
And help poor Andrew, and make this his home :
Thus, then arrang'd ; time now flew very fast,
And George's grievous hours were flown at last :
His sundry goods were ready for the van,

And he was now become an alter'd man.
The sun brought joy that usher'd in the day,
And so the hour when he was on the way :
For many a trial had fall'n to George's lot
Since he first occupied that little cot ;
But he had borne them all most patiently,
And never shrunk in his adversity
From that great duty, pray'r !—his great support,
His refuge in affliction, and resort.
    Farewell to Westonbury, and farewell
To cottage, garden, grunters, fowls, and all ;
In other hands their welfare now is cast,
And well for them if they 're as good 's the last !
" George Hollybrand "—they almost learn'd to speak,
But now he 's gone they 're doubly dumb and meek.
    Ten hours were told ; Jane listens to the wind,
Whose genial breathings thus impress'd her mind :
She fondly fancied that the breeze would bear
The far-off rumbling to her anxious ear ;
'T was not in vain—her fancy served her well,
As now the favouring winds bore up the vale
The welcome sound. · Ah ! who her joy could tell ?—
Yet happier still when she beheld the van
(At every pulse which beat) advancing on :
She waved her 'kerchief as it drew in sight,
And thus anticipated her delight ;
Her father answer'd the uplifted sign,
Then soon their tears with mutual scope combine,
For one more instant and a scene ensued
When the joy-liquid unprevented flowed.

CHAPTER THE FOURTH.

I.

Sweet twilight,—of all other hours most blest
For those whose prospect is their needed rest ;
When down the western sphere of heav'n had gone
The great and good—the all propitious sun.
Oh, Heaven ! how gracious is that mid-way hour,
When all the day-birds seek their somb'rous bow'r :
And when—if not in full—the quartering moon
Attracts the eye to the celestial zone,—
Such then the hour when George in lowly state
Trod erst the precincts of old Rollingate,
Where he was welcome—not by her alone,
Whom love begat and law decreed his own,
But every one, and one* among them all
Who had for years adorn'd the princely hall ;
She bade him happiness and kiss'd his hand,
And wrought her friendship with George Hollybrand :
Thus then.   And now the genial feast prepared
No longer waited but was meetly shared,
Till at a moderate hour they all repaired
To rest.   Joy reign'd supreme ; but with the morn
(Ah ! where the rose, there also thrives the thorn.)
Came grief ; for then the sadful news was borne
Of Andrew Hodge's death !—the dear old man
Had swoon'd, and died just at the hour of one ;
Death, monster evil, seem'd to 've long'd the hour
For his dark deed, and forced life's chamber-door :

* Aunt Toogood.

His awful mandate found n' opposing force
So in an instant Hodge was fell'd a corse.
    No longer would the poor old man relate
His thousand tales about dear Rollingate.
    No longer would he make his morning-call
And quaff the goblet in the " Servants' hall,"
Which he had done for many and many a year
And claim'd his usual " horn-and-half" of beer.
    Nor would he e'er interrogate again—
As he would call her—his " young Mistress Jane,"
And list to her sweet replicating word
When he would ask about his absent lord.
    No longer would the folks attending church
Behold him strutting through the western porch ;
Nor would the parson ever more espy
Old Andrew Hodge, with his auxiliar eye ;*
Nor would the children run again to meet
Him, all expectant of their Sunday sweet :—
No, no !—old Andrew now had breathed his last,
And all those trivial joys for ever past.

II.

Now, when the corpse to Appleton† was ta'en—
Among the mourners were "young Mistress Jane,"
And her dear father (by his daughter's side),
Who griev'd as though he had been long allied
To the departed ! but George Hollybrand
Ne'er had the joy to clasp old Andrew's hand

* A magnifying glass, which poor old Andrew was in the habit of using
when reading.
  † A little village, about a mile and a half from the lodge at Rollingate.

Before his spirit fled, for that same night
George came to Rollingate the soul took flight!—
And this sad sense of frail mortality,
Stung George's heart and wrung it bitterly.

O'er Andrew's grave a tablet-stone was rais'd ;
And as the sheep around about it graz'd
Arnold some day, perchance, might step thereon—
Himself to witness that the deed was done :
And, doubtless, if he lives to see the mound
A tear will trickle on that holy ground,
Where, near the spot (within the sacred fane),
Lord William's ancestors were deathful lain,—
So that no stranger would (when Arnold saw)
Be studious sorrowing o'er the dead below.

III.

Two Sabbaths, and ten days besides, gone by
Renewed the scope of pleasant memory ;
And now, 't was deem'd a prudent step to take—
That Hollybrand should comfortably make
The entrance-lodge his home, and take command
Of the subordinates about the land,—
Direct the labourers ; and survey the flock,
And keep at bay all interdicted stock.*

Much joy and comfort seem'd again in store
For Hollybrand, who once 'gan to deplore
Almost his own existence ; but now he
Saw in the future some felicity,—
And where his thanks were due, there they were pour'd,

---

* The cattle on adjacent farms.

And there his orizons unvarying soar'd.
   'Twas strange, but true—that George's birth-day fell
Upon the very day he went to dwell
(With full possession) in that pretty lodge,
Which so long shelter'd poor old Andrew Hodge :
Yes—it was so ; and always on this day
He kept a sort of sacred jubilee.
It seems, by record, that George Hollybrand was born
Some fifty years ago at Merrythorn,
Which place ('t is said, by those who 've sojourn'd
     there)
Had gain'd repute for its salubrious air ;
And George's father—Michael Hollybrand,
Own'd a small territ'ry of pasture-land ;
But owing to some law-suit he sustained —
Worse fortune for his son—was almost ruined :
His little portion, with regret, was sold
To meet th' opposing side's demand for gold.
(George, it appears, before to man was grown
Went forth to labour, and to earn his own.)
Thus then 't is hoped the prospects George now saw
Will counterbalance all his early woe.

IV.

The turnpike-road by which the cottage* stood
Led through a very picturesque neighbourhood,
In one direction, to the market-town,—
A place, for some-time past, of much renown,
And where the produce of this large estate—

---

* The lodge.

Excepting that required at Rollingate,
Was carted, and there sold as merchandise,
Which seldom ever fail'd to realise
The highest current price.   Now it was plann'd
The salesman, henceforth, should be Hollybrand,—
(For Cartwright* thought no man could better be
Adapted to this branch of sovereignty—
Besides a fit and proper personage
To buy and sell and labourers to engage ;
He also thought for sake of his dear child,
That George would see nought wasted or e'er spoil'd.)
So with th' assistance of young Martha Gray
(Old Andrew's niece), whom George engaged to stay.
He 'gan to feel at home, and soon became
Possessor of a moderate share of fame ;
Whilst Martha, who could read and write with ease,
Grew every day more studiously to please,
And would assist her master now and then
(When he required it) with her ready pen;—
Thus then when Hollybrand had to present
A statement of his dealings she, intent
Upon the subject, penn'd them most correct',—
As Cartwright seldom ever could detect
Aught wrong in the account, but should there be
The steward rectified it willingly.

Thus George, who scarcely ever had to do
With such important matters hitherto,
Became so skilful in the dealing art
That he was courted at the business mart—
Yes, so much so that he at last was ta'en

* Lord Arnold's steward.

As arbitrator and criterion :
And once-a-week for twenty years or more.
On Wednesdays at an usual early hour,
George to the township hied, there sold or bought :
His word was honor'd, and his custom sought.
   'T is fair to say—'T was not for that alone
That George was noted at this market town ;
But on account of Arnold's generousness—
His great regard for all their happiness ;
And—proof of this—it was their next intent,—
In illustration of their sentiment,
When he return'd home from the Continent,—
With unanimity to celebrate
Th' arrival of the Lord of Rollingate.
'T was rare indeed, but where there happ'd to be
A case, or cases, of real poverty
Made known to Arnold, p'rhaps by some good soul,
He ne'er demurr'd but instantly forestole
Their own anticipations with tenfold
Th' expected silver or expected gold ;
And to encourage the philanthropist—
If so invited—he would head the list,
And thus facilitate the needed crave—
To aid the living, or to find a grave
For some one dead, where were no means to pay ;
Or to support the annual holiday ;
According as the question might arise :
But should he e'er detect one in disguise
Soliciting his alms and feigning poor
He'd cast the wretch with vengeance from the door ;
Nor would begrudge t' uplift his shapely foot
And send the traitor reeling o'er—to boot.

V.

Returning home from market one dull day,
Unfortunately without company,
George came in contact with some vagrants, who—
When he approach'd—their trade began t' renew :
One of the ruffians, dreadful in his look,
From 'neath his ragged coat a pistol took
And aimed it straight at George's breast, and said—
" Give us your money or I'll shoot you dead !"
Poor George, replying to the impulse, drew
His bag and gave it to the fiendish crew
(For there were four surrounded him, so he
Could not resist their hellish mimicry ;
But felt content, as 't were, to avoid the strife—
Which in their direful hearts was plainly rife),
Most thankful that the villains spared his life.
    One of the brigands made all progress vain,
Another counted o'er the ravish'd gain,
The others in the rear ransack'd the cart,
Then, all uniting, off the ruffians start ;
But dreamt not justice was so near at hand—
When at its bar each vagabond would stand
Confronted with the victim of the scene,
Besides a witness who, by chance, within
Th' adjacent field, beheld and heard them urge
Their method of attack upon poor George ;
Who saw the fray accomplishèd, and fled
To give instructions of the direful deed,—
Which subsequently led to their arrest
And their removal o'er the ocean's breast.

VI.

Now, loit'ring in a wood, they stay'd till night
Avail'd them for their unmolested flight,
And then sought refuge in a roadside-inn ;
Where the carousal scarcely did begin
Ere some great noise excites the villains' fear—
They 're startled ! therefore try to disappear.
But there remain'd no shadow of a chance ;
For six determined officers advance
And seize them.   But what next ensued ?—
They aim resistance, and with clubs of wood
Assail the constables with awful rage ;
Who, in return, assiduously engage
In direful conflict, and at length subdue
The barb'rous and antagonistic crew :—
The word " Surrender," fraught with dreadful threat,
With due submission instantly was met.
    Thus, then, o'erpower'd, dejected, and dismay'd,
Like sheep to slaughter they were instant led—
With handcuff'd wrists—each to a felon's cell,
Where they awaited their disastrous trial.

VII.

When George, that dismal eve, at home arrived,
With much emotion he sat down and cried ;
But, having always on his God relied,
He thank'd th' Almighty that the hand was stay'd,
Which at one moment threaten'd to have laid
Him low.   Gray then observ'd a something, which

Made her unhappy, so with anxious speech
Besought her Master, thus : " Sir, pray thee—why
Art thou so sad?"   George wiped his tearful eye
And answered her :—" Ah ! Gray, I'm back again,
But coming homeward four unholy men
Molested me and took my cash, and more—
The rogues decamp'd with all our weekly store."

Those words had scarce escaped poor George's lips
When he was struck with the advancing steps
As of a horse ('t was now just nine o'clock) ;
And then obedient to a hurried knock
The door was open'd, and a voice enquired
If master Hollybrand had yet retired
To rest.   "Oh ! no, Sir," Gray replied, " he 's not."
" Will you be kind enough to say that Scott,*" * * *
George knew the voice and hasten'd to receive
The man of order, vengeance, or reprieve :
He said.   Now finding that the men were ta'en,
George felt reliev'd from an oppressive strain ;
And on the following morning, by command,
He went to prosecute th' inhuman band,—
He strode his pony at the hour of nine,
To be in attendance at th' appointed time.

When near the place where they attack'd him, there
George saw the fragments of some earthenware,—
A portion of his stores,—which in their haste
The robbers had incautiously laid waste :
As may be well conceived—just at this spot,
George ponder'd sadly o'er the direful plot ;
But yet rejoiced to think what had befell

* Chief of the constabulary force at Ruttendell.

The treacherous vagabonds at Ruttendell.*
So he proceeded, and, when he had gain'd
The Justice' Court, beheld all four arraign'd ;
Who, when they saw the prosecutor there,
Hung down their heads in deep and sad despair :
No doubt their hearts were wrung, and well they might
When they observ'd their unpropitious plight,—
Especially he who beckon'd on the rest,
And held the pistol straight to George's breast :
The one who had received a sabre-cut
Sat moaning piteously with eyes half shut,—
For on his thigh the cutlass made a gash,
And struck the bone beneath an inch of flesh :
In years of youth the others seem'd to be,
Who had forsook the path of honesty—
Intent on mischief and misrule, but now
Remorse and horror sat upon their brow.
God grant them mercy ! but the law decreed
That England of such demons should be freed ;
And so in time all four were sent away
To end their lifetime in old " Bot'ny Bay,"—
The merited reward of infamy.

VIII.

When Jane, as usual, took her Thursday tour,
And reach'd the lodge about th' eleventh hour —
A plan her loving temper had devised
For both their comfort—she was much surprisèd
And much alarm'd—nay, felt a bit unwell

* The market town, before alluded to.

When Gray epitomised the fraughtful tale ;
But at the glad intelligence that they—
The robbers—were secure in custody,
Besides the message George had left behind
To comfort and appease his daughter's mind,
Her sorrow'd countenance lit up anew,
Her placid cheeks regain'd their healthful hue ;
And she became composed : yet the alloy—
Suspense combined with deep anxiety
(Those dubious moments which must intervene
Before her father could reach home again),—
Compell'd poor Jane to shed a transient tear,
And to extemporise a passing prayer.
    Some hours elapsed in this unenvied mood,
Till Martha's warbler* (in its hall of wood),
Rang out its watchful note, as it was wont
Whenever any one approach'd the front,—
And never fail'd save when the darksome night
Would press its weight upon its tender sight,—
So Jane depended, and away she flew
And found the pretty angel telling true :
Wide swung the gate, and ere another breath
(Profound and solemn as the hour of death),
Jane clasp'd her father's hand, and bade him say
What were the fortunes of the current day.
He 'kiss'd her cheek and smilingly replied
(Although emotion, for awhile, denied
His pregnant tongue) - "'T is well, dear Jane, 'tis
        well !
Much sympathy prevails at Ruttendell,

---

* A canary bird.

For this sad loss; but great shall be the praise
To Him above, who hath prolong'd my days;
For at one moment in that dreadful hour
My pulse forsook its regulated pow'r,
And I, my dear, expected—sad to say—
To have been launch'd into eternity!—
Yes—thanks to God, whose providence disposed
The dreadful deed those horrid men proposed,
And prompted me, when life seem'd but a wave,
To yield the substance of the villains' crave."

George housed his pony, and return'd to " tea,"
And pass'd this evening far more cheerfully
Than the preceding one, and happily felt
(At length) somewhat atoned by the result;
Nor was dear Jane less comforted than he
For this escape from a calamity,—
As such it would have been (I dare to state)
For some considerable time at Rollingate;
And whilst they liv'd time never could erase
Their recollection of the painful case.

IX.

Now Jane, perceiving it was getting late,
Ceased for this evening to interrogate,
And bade them both a favourable good night;
Then hasten'd home, maturing as she went
The manner of depicting the event
To her dear aunt, and how t' explain away—
Without alarm—the cause of her delay;
Which she accomplishèd with praiseworthy tact,
By slowly unfolding the momentous fact,—

And so unburden'd her invaded breast;
Wept—but for joy—and then retired to rest.
    But many a day Jane felt (poor girl!) unfit
To undertake her lessons, and would sit
Apparently in fear lest aught should mar—
By some catastrophe to him afar—
Her own anticipations, and destroy
Their mutual bodings of conjugal joy:
She'd read his letters (and give each a kiss),
In which, alone, she found a world of bliss;
And oftentimes a tear would damp her face
Whilst she replaced them in her writing-case.
    On one occasion, when Jane heard the lark's
Blithe carolling, she made these sweet remarks—
" Ah! little minstrel of the air so free,
None of thy kindred can discourse like thee;
Whilst list'ning to thy solo—charming thing—
I long to be a bird to choose thee king;
If so, I'd crown thee with pure wreaths of gold,
And then adventurously would make so bold
To claim thy friendship; yes, and seek thy love:
It may be thou art he that Arnold strove
One day so perseveringly to catch,
But thou, O! songster, proved too good a match."
    Another time, whilst sitting studiously
Beneath the branches of a stately tree,
The cuckoo 'lighted on its topmost limb,
And, as his wont, his simple notes would chime
Melodiously; which fell upon Jane's ear—
That, like a statue, she sat fix'd, for fear
The slightest movement might affright her guest,
And thus disturb the darling's transient rest:

So much delighted was dear Jane to hear
The meek enchanter piping forth so clear
Its rare alternate notes, that she could not
Refrain rememb'ring Westonbury cot :
But when the cuckoo left its perch and fled
Across the vale, Jane lifted up her head,
Exclaiming—" Oh, thou trumpeter of May !
I've sat in pain, almost, that thou should'st stay,
Yet thou hast flown ; fie on thee, timid bird:"
But ere she'd time to speak another word
She, hearing footsteps as of something near,
Turn'd quickly round and saw an antler'd deer,
Of graceful form, the noblest of his race,
Matchless in stature, and lord of the chase :
Jane's movements made the handsome creature bound,
Light as an angel, o'er the scythèd ground :
" Ah ! nimble forester," she said, " I see—
'T was you that drove the cuckoo off the tree."

X.

A year and seven months had now gone by
Since Arnold Mountjoy left for Germany :
Each new epistle borne across the main
Brought tidings of increasing love for Jane,—
Entreating her, " Be constant ; for my sake
Shun company,—at least, take care to make
Acquaintance only with my choicest friends ;
Be chaste, for chastity with virtue blends :
Thy tutors, dearest, write me pleasing notes,—
Such as I send thee now :" so, on he quotes—
　　*　　　*　　　*　　　*　　　*　　　*

And naturally felt—if half of this were truth—
How clever would she 've been if, in her youth,
She had been educated by degrees
At one of England's best academies.

Now he began to contemplate with pride
A happy meeting with his future bride ;
He even fix'd the month, nay, very hour
For setting out upon his homeward tour :
(And those acquainted with this noble man
Knew how precise he 'd execute his plan :)—
" Five silvery moons must run their course," he said,
" Before I take her to the nuptial bed ;
Day, godly flame, will fire the orient strand
Three months or more ere I shall reach the land,
Where, O, blest country—bounded by the sea,
I thank my God there is a home for me !"—
And as the wheel of age roll'd swiftly by
He penn'd th' epistle which should intimate
The day he hoped t' arrive at Rollingate.

.

XI.

Obedient to the Hand which governs heav'n—
The Power by which the spacious earth is driv'n,
Round roll'd this mighty globe with awful speed ;
The virgin moon perform'd her holy deed—
Reflecting God's undeviating light,
Which gives us day, while she attends the night.

At length Jane Hollybrand, expectant, saw—
Though to her sorrow, coming very slow'—
The bumpkin postman, who appear'd intent
On solving some rude myst'ry as he went ;

And then, as fate would have it, stopp'd to see
If he could work it out 'rithmetic'lly,—
Threw down his bag, regardless of its worth,
And sat himself upon dear Mother Earth ;
There bask'd, as 't were, full in old Horus' eye,
Whilst she, expecting him,* could almost cry—
So sad was this suspense ; but when he came,
The joy she felt relieved the man from blame.

Now her sweet features glowed with ruddy hue,
And as she read the letter through and through
She seem'd to pause at one particular place,
And raised her handkerchief towards her face,—
No doubt 't was done t' obstruct the lucent tear,
Urged on perceiving that the time drew near
For her espousal, and that happy hour
When love, unhamper'd, delegates its pow'r.

'Mong other things (momentous as a whole)
He gave instructions that the central-hall
Should be re-decorated, and elsewhere—
Which needed it—to undergo repair.

He lovingly express'd a great desire
That Jane, at once, should choose her own attire,—
" Have every necessary thing," he wrote, "complete
Mind not the cost, my love, but be discreet ;
Bid dear Aunt Toogood do the same, and lo !
See that she gets her locks† curl'd up anew :
Let Slash (the coachman) and old honest John‡
Get each a suit, and neatly fitted on ;—
In fact, the servants all, each in their sphere,
Must on that day in wedding-garb appear :

* The postman.   † Artificial tresses.
‡ John Somers, the head groom.

And now, dear Jane, the last and not the least—
Invite your father to the marriage-feast,—
Tell him, my darling, I 'll require his aid,
And hope, some day, to see him well repaid ;
Ask him to name, when next he goes to ' town,'*
To my familiar friend, Sir Humphrey Brown,
And his good Lady, that (if all goes well)
I hope to pass again through Ruttendell
About the middle of the month ensuing
(The anniversary month of my first wooing) :
I find, at Dover, I 'll arrive too late
To catch the coach ; so will communicate
From thence to you, dear Jane ; will also write
To dear Sir H——, and give him an ' invite.' "

XII.

Now when Sir Humphrey heard this welcome news
He said, for joy, " God bless my buckle-shoes,"†
And to his wife—" I think, dear Lady B——,
Betwixt your loyal ladyship and me,
There is no time to lose—so I 'll go down
And have an interview with Champernown : "‡
He went : and soon a numerous gathering
Propounded measures for a welcoming ;
Which (came to pass with almost regal state)
Greeted the noble Lord of Rollingate :—
The streets were spann'd with flags of every shade,

---

* Ruttendell.

† A quaint expression which Sir H. B. had acquired when any new sentiment of pleasure inspired his heart.

‡ Mr. Frederick Champernown, stationer and news-agent.

Bearing the mottoes of each goodly trade ;
From door to door were planted shrubs and flowers,
Transforming houses into Sylvan bowers
Six furlongs distant 'rose t' endear the eye,*
Two triple arches ; each one bore on high
A crimson banner ring'd with bullion gold ;
Whose meet inscriptions adequately told
(In silvery letters, more than tongue can tell)
Th' excessive joy which reign'd at Ruttendell.

CHAPTER THE FIFTH.

I.

WHEN now (that morn) Aurora ope'd the course,
And Sol strode forth, eight charmers bid discourse ;
Their firstling-notes, borne on the balmy breeze,
Bestirr'd the rooks in the adjacent trees ;
" Ring, ting, ting, tong, this is our song,"—say they—
To rouse ye sleepers for the holiday :
A thousand flues erst wind their dingy smoke ;
Whilst children run, half nude, to have a look,
And listen to the mimic guns as they
Peal forth applausive of th' auspicious day :
The streets are now invaded by gay youths
Prebent already on the comfit booths ;
And as the morning grows show signs of love
Whilst sauntering through the artificial grove :
The gentry-residents command the throng,

* At each end of the town.

And at the time appointed march along
Towards the bound'ry, there (some frolicking)
They 'wait th' arrival of their local king.

II.

He comes, he comes : hurrahs denote the deed ;
And then harmoniously the host proceed
With pompous pride, concordant, through the town,
In meet obedience to Sir Humphrey Brown,
Who marshall'd them ; and as they onward march--
In civil order 'neath the banner'd arch—
Loud shouts of triumph reach the distant car,
And loud hurrahs responsive fill the air.
Full sixty horses, led the fairy way,
Adorn'd with choice rosettes, in meet array ;
Each favour'd beast bore on its gladsome guest,
In twenty rows arear, and three abreast :
Then follow'd Tympanum,* the lord of sound,
And his train'd band, which shook the very ground ;
They blew their instruments so mighty loud
It drown'd the chorus of the motley crowd.
Next, came Lord Mountjoy, in his chaise-and-four,
Waving his hat obeisant to the poor,
The maim'd, the aged, who belined the street ;
Who with huzzas the noble stranger greet :
Among the townsfolk, marching in the line,
A hornpipe-dancer, bacchus'd up with wine—
Or some commodity—with healthful pride,
Timed out his joy with his Brazilian hide.

* The drum.

Some gentle ladies, at a branching street,
Had ('midst some evergreens, arrang'd so neat
As to attract Lord Arnold's searching eye)
Affix'd a sentence—which was, by-the-bye,
Nought less than this : "God bless Jane Holly-
    brand." (!)
He saw it, 'rose ; and, silencing the band,
Gave forth the signal for three loud hurrahs
For those young damsels, and their sweet mammas ;
Sir Humphrey saw, and held his 'kerchief out,
And urged this beacon for another shout—
'T was done : and then Lord Mountjoy spoke aloud :
" I thank you, ladies, for I 'm very proud
Indeed to see, this day, my choice approved ;
I do assure you that my heart is moved :
Some future time I hope 't will be my fate,
My joy, to welcome you at Rollingate."
    Going by the church, the band clash'd with the
        bells ;
Which, with the cannons' boom at intervals—
And oft—produced the most discordant sounds,
Resembling yells of hungry kennell'd hounds.
    At length the second archway strikes the eye :
The glossy banner, stretch'd across the sky,
Reveal'd those sacred words—" God give him health."
(Now, as 't was certain Arnold lack'd not wealth,
Nought else could typify, to that extent,
Their love, as this spontaneous compliment.)
    Then forth three furlongs from the sylvan grove,
He bade adieu, and hasten'd to his love.
    The host return'd, and banqueted the poor,
And much rejoicing reign'd till a late hour.

III.

Far in the west, the clouds were gathering fast
About the space in the celestial vast,
Where the great 'Trav'ler takes his eve's repast.—
That famed dispenser of eternal light,
Who bathes his rosy form in depths of night,
And bids the world behold him gently steep
His swollen body in the radiant deep;—
There, like a whale beneath the liquid main,
Retires in confidence; and comes again
Refresh'd, and strengthen'd, for returning day:
But he, unlike the monsters of the sea,
Whose days are number'd, shall for ever rise—
For ever wander through th' unbounded skies!
   Two hours, or nearly, Horus had to march,
Ere he could reach the buttress of the arch
Which spans the ocean of ethereal air:
There, cloudlings waited for the golden fare—
That unmatch'd crimson, to edge round the robes—
The night apparel of the king of globes.

IV.

When Arnold gain'd the summit of the hill
(Where stood the ruins of an ancient mill),*
The last uprising on his homeward course,
And where the village baker came for gorse.
Conveying it in paniers, on his horse
(For in abundance on the hill it grew).

---

* A windmill.

The turrets of his mansion 'rose to view :
Then did his noble heart within him leap ;
And when he first beheld the grazing sheep,
In those prolific slopes, down in the vale
(Where many a hunter's blast had rode the gale—
Whilst in pursuit of the despairing fox,
And where Sir Humphrey and Sir Edward Knox
Had often tried the mettle of their steeds,
With Arnold's father's ——, 'cross those daisy-meads,
And woodland-acres, and yon distant Down,
Where nimble Reynards for their lives had flown) ;
Then did Lord Arnold picture to his mind
His lovely Jane, so beautiful and kind.
But yet he had to traverse o'er a mile
Before he could behold the beam, the smile,
The tender tear of joy ; and hear that voice
Articulate the language of his choice :—
" Ah ! Slash,"* he said, " I see the pale-blue smoke,
From the Lodge-chimney, 'scending through the oak."
    Five minutes more, the horses gently swerve,
And canter gracefully, around the curve,
Through the Lodge-gateway ; there stood Hollybrand,
As meek as ever, with his hat in hand :
Arnold saluted him with right good will,—
" I 'd hoped to 've seen you in at Ruttendell ;
How is it, George, you were not there to-day,
Astride your pony, with my tenantry ? "
George modestly replied—" I thought, good Sir,
My greatest comfort would be first to hear
Thy welcome voice near to my sacred home ! "

* The coachman.

" And are you happy?"   " Yes," he said.   " Then
      come,
Secure the gate, and make your dwelling right ;
And spend an hour with us at home to-night."

V.

Up on a hill, about three furlongs off,
The stable-boy (not far from being a dwarf)
Was sent by Jane, and caution'd how to raise
And wave on high a strip of scarlet baize,
So soon as he beheld his master's chaise.
(A beacon-signal to the anxious Jane,
Whilst she sat peeping through the window pane ;
For on this hill a distant view arose
Of the high-road, 'long which the traveller goes
When journeying to and fro near Ruttendell.)
Jane saw the streamer rais'd ! then knew full well
Her lover soon would be within her sight ;
She wept for joy, so great was her delight.
   The south-west breeze bore up the greenwood vale
The chaise's rattle,—thanks to the sweet gale :
An instant more the whistling whip was heard :
Jane look'd, and lo ! across the grassy sward
She saw the moving mass advancing swift ;—
No longer of her love is she bereft !
   (Dear Mistress Toogood fired her aged breast ;
And, venturing forth to meet the lordly guest
Beneath the portico,—dress, " bishop-sleeved,"—
Bestowed her saintly blessings ; thus relieved
Her dear old heart of two years' sobs and sighs ;

Yet even then she scarce believed her eyes,
For seventy years and five had made them dim ;
But when she heard his voice she knew 't was him !)

VI.

On came the carriage : Arnold drops the reins ;
Descends, and instantly his love entwines—
Dumb with emotion at his kind embrace.
Whilst gentle drops stole down Jane's blushing face,
Lord Arnold's own bright eyes, keen to behold,
'Came dimm'd with joy : yes ! could he but have told
One half the feelings wrought upon his heart,
Not even then a tithe could he impart :
He saw, at once, her tutors, when they wrote,
Had partially concealed how they were smote ;—
Not, as he naturally might have inferr'd—
That they 'd contriv'd to please him, and conferr'd
One with another : no, this was n't the case,
For he beheld her now endowed with grace ;
Her comeliness and rare symmetral form
Surpass'd his hope, and 'flam'd his bosom warm.
  Recovering from this reverie of bliss,
Jane spoke in silvery tones ; her tale was this—
" I 've learn'd to love thee, in thy absence, dear ;
Pray pardon me, if now I love thee here ;"
So placed her hand immediately in his,
And seal'd his lips with her first earnest kiss.
Arnold, in raptures with this stroke of love,
Glimpsed her two joys ; and envied not high Jove !

VII.

At eight o'clock, Jane's father had arrived :
With all his power he zealously contrived,
But fail'd, to be excused from the repast ;
And therefore, being prevail'd upon at last,
He dined, for the first time, with his good lord ;
Dear Jane assisting him with her kind word.
('T was now too late for Toogood to be there,
As habit had compell'd her to repair
Unto her bedroom, for the night's repose.)
The cloth remov'd, Lord Arnold, quite jocose,
Related one of his adventurous tales,
In which the plunder of some foreign mails
Form'd part the story : Jane felt much amused ;
But Hollybrand himself appear'd confused ;
As though assured, by its similitude,
His own mishap was really understood :
Then Arnold, in his wonted happy mood,
Perceiving Hollybrand confounded, smil'd,
And said to George : " It is your own dear child
Who sent me tidings of that dread affair ;
I'll lay a wager, George, you 've taken care,
When going to town upon a market-day,
To guard against a similar affray !"
" Yes, yes," said George, with smiling countenance,
" You may depend, dear sir, I've ever since
Ta'en this precaution—never more to start
To Ruttendell, alone, with horse and cart."
    Then Arnold, after this tale, told in jest,
Touch'd on the subject which his heart lov'd best,—

Of making dearest Jane his loving wife ;
" On whom," he said, " depends my love of life."

VIII.

A serious conversation then ensued—
The retrospect and future well reviewed—
Lord Arnold delicately sought to name
The nuptial-day, and urg'd the blushing Jane
To fix the date ; but she, with subdued voice,
Begg'd courteously to be excused,—" the choice,"
She softly said, " dear Arnold, should be thine ;
And what your wish may be, that shall be mine."
He then, most fondly, kiss'd her modest cheek,
And named it for the following Wednesday-week :
" Shall it be so ?" he said * * * " come, dear, express
Thy pleasure, and enhance my happiness !"
She press'd his hand, and breathed the mono-word *
To which George Hollybrand at once concurr'd :
And silently pour'd forth this orison,—
" O righteous God, bless Thou this gen'rous man !"

IX.

Sleep's slumbering influence now began to fall,
And Arnold must have felt it most of all,—
The day had been a double-day to him ;
His dark blue eye had lost its sparkling beam
(And only those who pass through similar scenes,—
Who are the objects of such welcomin's,—

* Yes !

Can comprehend one half th' attendant pain,
Extreme of pleasure forces on the brain).
Night now had enter'd in th' eleventh hour.
The sun was on his antipodal tour;
But heav'n was not forsaken by its queen,
For she was silv'ring o'er th' expansive green; *
With all her wonted grace she shed her rays,
And number'd this as one of her bright days;
She lit the path, in which George had to roam,
That he, in safety, might regain his home:
Each other bade adieu; George homeward sped;
And Arnold Mountjoy sought his lonely bed.
(Twelve other nights, he † knew, must be bygone,—
Twelve other suns must cross the temperate zone,—
Ere her ‡ virginity—which by the law
Is reckon'd sacred—shall be broken through.)
Jane had retir'd; her evening pray'rs were flown;
A snow-white pillow form'd her peaceful crown.
The night was still; all Nature seem'd to lull;
And God, alone, the guardian of the hall!

    Thus closed a day, one of unusual mirth,—
One more fleet joy, on this revolving earth.

X.

Again great Horus, the vanguard of day,
Rolls up th' horizon, and paints o'er the sky.

    Eight harvest labourers bask on yonder hill,
Partaking of their early breakfast-meal;
Refresh'd they rise and scythe the bearded corn.

---

    * The Park.   † Arnold.   ‡ Jane.

And nurse it till 't is ready for the barn :
From field to field the sickle rushes forth ;
The master * meditates upon its worth :
He bushels it, and bags it in a cart,
And takes it to a profitable mart ;
Receives the coin, and cheers his trusty heart.
    But while those peasants laid the hill-side bare,
The mansion inmates had their daily care ;
And Rollingate was now all joy within,
Preparing for the matrimonial scene.
The different tradesfolk came from Ruttendell
With their resources for the festival ;
And stores of every kind were now being brought.
(The wedding-ring already had been wrought.)
Upholsterers were busily at work
From early morning till the day grew dark :
Two suites of rooms were thus being re-arranged ;
And sundry goods appropriately changed.
(Arnold, himself, took special interest—
Observing everything done in its best.)
Three decorators, from one Mr. Small's——
Were renovating ceilings, doors, and walls.

XI.

The country jew'ler † made an extra call,
And urged his trinkets for the coming ball ;
Round to the back, ‡ he plied his hollow trash,
And smil'd in secret as he told the cash.
(The cunning fellow thought this was, of course,

---

   * The proprietor.   † A hawker of watches and jewellery.
      ‡ Among the servants.

A splendid chance, some of his wares to force ;—
He guess'd aright—for housemaids, cooks, and scullion
Bought his mosaic, contentedly, for bullion.)
A genteel " Packman," * who for years had made
His regular calls, now, following up his trade
With silks, and satins, cottons, every shade—
Avowing cheapness, with a wondrous knack—
Consid'rably reduced his holy pack :
All gather'd 'round him with an earnest zeal :
His India silks, if not, were looking real :
So one and all, including old John Swift,†
Bought something of the man before he left,—
Determin'd were they to be prim and gay
Upon their noble master's wedding-day.

XII.

The fattest buck which trod the vast domain
Was for the banquet seasonably slain ;
And choice provisions, of the daintiest sort
(Full meet to grace the table for the court),
Were being selected with the greatest care
By one‡ who was himself a connoisseur.

    Day after day had flown with magic haste ;
The banquet-room was 'ranged with nicest taste ;
And everything throughout seem'd neat and clean
(Fit for the habitation of a queen).

---

* A wandering draper.
† John Swift, a very old servant (formerly coachman) of Arnold's father ;
who still was an inmate of the mansion, though almost incapable of doing
any kind of work.
‡ Lord Mountjoy.

All invitations had been duly sent ;
Lord Arnold look'd quite happy and content :
Naught now remain'd but to pluck fresh the flowers,
And plant the banners on the two high towers.

CHAPTER THE SIXTH.

I.

HAIL, happy morn ! Aurora ope'd the gate ;
And made a passage for heav'n's potentate—
The harbinger of joy, in grand estate ;
Who for awhile appear'd inclined to halt—
To see if any, but found not a fault :
His beams had beckon'd forth the spotless bride ;
Her virgin nightcap she had thrust aside.
God only saw her as she doff'd her gown :
No human eye beheld her kneeling down :
None, but the Almighty, heard her fervent pray'rs :
No earthly being could see her faithful tears.
(Enough ! enough !—come, check thy heaving breast :
Sigh not, fond maiden,—lovers have no rest
Ere they have some one to share half their fate ;
And thou art chosen for that happy state.)
    Courage commanded her—" rise, gentle maid!"
Her heart felt lighter, and her tears were stay'd.
    *   *   *   *   *
Virtue's reward :—say, Jove, what is the prize ?—
What canst thou give ? what can ye realise
Sufficiently in value for this maid,—
Whose tongue ne'er yet had even utterèd

One vulgar sentence, one blasphemous word, —
Who never lov'd before she lov'd her lord?

II.

Half-after-eight,* clad in a rich pale green,†
And looking like a lovely fairy-queen,
(If such a creature e'er on earth was seen,)
Jane came down stairs ; there, waiting at the foot,
Her lover greeted her with this salute—
He sanctified her with a bridegroom's kiss ;
The bride return'd it, —thus a twofold bliss.
A hasty breakfast they in peace partook,
And subsequently scann'd the godly-book ;
A sacred feeling fill'd each anxious breast :
Then, for awhile, they parted to get drest.‡
Punctual, at ten—George Hollybrand came in.
(Methinks how proud Jane's father must have been
On that bright morning, to behold his own   *   *   *
Oh ! think ye not that many a tear had stol'n
Down o'er his fiftied cheeks, ere he had ta'en
His early meal, a-thinking of dear Jane?)
Toogood, (dear creature, busy as a bee,
For one so old,—yea, nimble as a flea,)
Seem'd now as though her life was e'en at stake,
Adjusting flowers around the bridal-cake ;
A massive silver stand supports it up ;
Beside it, stood an ancient golden cup,—
Engrav'd with Bacchus, riding on a ram,—
In which a thousand purple streams had swam.

---

* O'clock.   † A green dress.   ‡ To put on the wedding-garments.

(O goblet, could'st thou tell but half the mirth
Which thou alone hast witnessed on earth !
Ah ! could'st thou tell whose lips have kiss'd thy rim,
When festive-wine 'had fill'd thee to the brim !
No, no, thou canst not ; but thou art here still,
As ever ready for thy sumptuous fill :
To-day, in thy proud bosom there will shine
Repeated bumpers of the rarest wine ;
To-day, thy lordly owner will pass round
The festive board, thy majesty profound ;
Thy sides shall quiver with harmonious sound.)

III.

Time flies apace ; the marriage-scene begins :
Sir Humphrey, and his two grand-daughters, (twins,)
Two fair-hair'd damsels, draped in richest blond,—
Of whom, Sir Humphrey was extremely fond,—
Had just arriv'd.   (It should, just here, be said
That Lady Brown was now an invalid ;
And, consequently, she could not be there ;
But sent her blessings to the happy pair.)
Loud rang the old-hall bell, announcing plain—
Some gentle-folk, an entrance sought to gain :
At once Lord Mountjoy, (smiles upon his face,)
Sped forth to greet them ; with admiring grace,
And noble bearing, Arnold usher'd in
The wedding guests unto his own dear queen.
   Jane had been seated, but she now was ris'n,
And look'd an angel just escaped from heav'n :
Her dark brown tresses form'd her diadem ;
Her eyes surpass'd in radiancy, the gem

Which shone upon her bosom.   (O ! ye gods,
And queenly nymphs, who dwell in sylvan woods—
If such there are—come hither, if so bold
To hazard such a step, for here behold !
Not Venus, nor one vassal of the sky,
With all their graces, can in form outvie
Jane Hollybrand.   Nor can that mighty Jove,
Who reigns by courtesy in realms above,—
Whom all the suns, and moons, of heav'n adore,—
Whose charms subdued the heathen hordes of war,—
Can find a virgin equal to compare !)

IV.

Precisely as the clock dealt out eleven,
And all the hosts assembled—who were bidden—
Had 'fresh'd their bodies and each loving-soul,
They wend their way into the entrance-hall ;
Thence to the front, where the first coach doth stand,
Awaiting famed Sir Humphrey, Jane, and Hollybrand:
When they were seated and prepared to start,
The second coach draws up, which (quite as smart)
Receives Lord Arnold Mountjoy, and beside
Those pretty twins,*—attendants on the Bride :
The third, and last, contain'd Sir Edward Knox,
His wife, and daughter, in rare silken-frocks
With whom, dear Mistress Toogood found a seat,
And thus the bridal-party is complete.
An instant more they 're on the happy road
To seal the contract in the house of God,

---

* Sir Humphrey's two daughters.

Where crowd the villagers,—some 'round the porch,
And some within the flint-embedded* church,
Where they, expectant, 'wait the hour to see
The heroine of the day's festivity.

v.

The merry charmers, with their brazen tongues,
Make efforts to chime forth their favourite songs,—
Till the bold ringers are inform'd—that now
They must await until the nuptial vow
Is sanction'd by the law. Now every eye
Is bent towards the road, where they espy
Sir Humphrey's carriage coming up the " green ; "
And hail the occupants, who are therein :
Then, close behind, another coach appears ;
The villagers send forth unbounded cheers ;—
They doff their neckerchiefs, and aught beside
Spontaneously to greet the beauteous Bride :
Sir Edward follows, with two handsome " greys,"
Outvieing in stature old Sir Humphrey's " bays."

VI.

The sacred pile is reach'd ; its chancel trod ;
Around the altar, all in sight of God
Are reverently kneeling * * * Then they rise,
And one, there is, had need to wipe her eyes ;—
This is that gentle one, who 's made a wife ;—
Now Lady Mountjoy, for her mortal life !
        *   *   *   *   *

---

* The exterior masonry.

The ceremony's o'er; the bells peal out;
The villagers, again, raise high a shout.
    Beneath a tree 'n the centre of the "green,"
A fiddle, flute, and a bass-violin,
Surrounded by a motley group, are playing
That well-adapted tune—"Haste to the wedding."
Lord Arnold beckon'd to the "master man;"*
Whose hurry overturn'd the liquor-can!
His great misfortune soon is set aright,
By something pleasing to the fiddler's sight;
For which he bowed: but, quickly turning 'round,
He tripp'd; and, falling sideways on the ground,
Smash'd in the "belly" of his instrument;
The wondering crowd burst out in merriment:
Himself, unhurt, beheld the mischief done,
And swore, with vengeance, on the "evil-one."
(This self-conceited Jullien of the band,
Remember'd long the name of Hollybrand.)

VII.

Now, undesirous to prolong the tale—
By repetition what at Ruttendell
Was being enacted to commemorate
Th' event, I'll beg the reader back to Rollingate;
There, 'neath the portico, sweet flowers were laid
Promiscuously, to bear the lightsome tread
Of that pure virgin's unstain'd wax-like form,
As yet a stranger to the inherent storm.
    Lord Arnold had decreed that, on this day,

* The leader of the band.

His labourers, servants, and his tenantry,
Should be partakers of the marriage-feast ;
So 'round the stately doorway, there each guest,
(Of course—not one, but wore their very best,)
Full fifty, stood in regular marshall'd keep,
Cheering, most lustily, her ladyship,
As she alighted from the stately chaise,
And, like a fairy, trod the crimson baize,—
Which, on the doorsteps, had been placed with care
In the hour's absence of the nuptial pair.

VIII.

The banquet-board is spread in bounteous style,
And every face around it bears a smile ;
With fruit and flowers the hall is well perfumed :
The bridal-cake's dealt out ; the goblet's toomed,
And all is harmony : joy's dominant :
Within, the very walls seem resonant—
As with the echoings of gay scenes of yore ;
But none had ever equall'd this before.
    From noon, until the solemn midnight-hour,
Heaven vouchsafed one unabated show'r
Of mirthfulness, of prudent revelry,
Of one enchanting scene of gaiety ;
Such as will be historical.

IX.

Then gracious Somnus, with his nightly spell,
(Beneath whose mystic beams great monarchs bend,)

Proclaim'd—the festival was at an end :
The good old god, who ever-timely wise,
Trod on the tender covering of their eyes ;
And bade them pay due homage unto night :
But there was one, (the god dimm'd not his sight,)
Whose breast was blazing with that nuptial flame,
Which strives to ancestralize a family name ;
His sweet companion, buckling for the deed,
Encourag'd him t' advance : her love obey'd :
Fair Bapta,* charitably, drew her veil,
And bade the loving warriors doff their mail,—
'T was done !—they waver'd, for the shock was great,
The conflict ceas'd.   Concordia,† reign'd in state.

      *   *   *   *   *

And when another summer-time had flown,
(For God had bless'd the mould wherein 'twas sown,)
The gladsome father, named his own, his own. . .

      *   *   *   *   *

"Virtue rewarded :"—be ye all discreet ;
For love, without discretion, courts defeat.

---

* Bapta, the goddess of shame.   † Concordia, the goddess of peace.

IN CONCLUSION.

A Word for Gifford.

A word for Gifford,* ere I close my book ;
For only recently I had a look—
As chance would have it†—at his wondrous pile,
And then for joy each couplet drew a smile ;
But what beside?—regret I had not seen
Before th' effusions of his fraughtful pen.

    *   *   *   *   *

A word for Gifford, ("last, but not the least,")—
Whose rare productions ‡ were the surest test
Of his bright mind ; then why do I attempt
Panegyric, (and gain, perhaps, contempt
For my poor self,) when such as Byron write—
Expressive of their pleasure and delight—
In praise of him? 'T is—that I can't withhold
My little instrument, which seems so bold
As to presume to dictate to my muse—
" It is a duty ! therefore dare n't refuse."

    *   *   *   *   *

* William Gifford was born at Ashburton, April, 1756, and, as may be inferred from the fact of his being interred at Westminster Abbey, attained a celebrity of no common order.

† This may appear singular, and unpardonable, but the Author (of this little work) is obliged to confess that it was only within a few days prior to the publication of these poems he, by accident, (having purchased a small volume in the Strand, London,) for the first time had the pleasure of perusing a portion of the works of this great man.

‡ His satirical poems,—the " Baviad," and "Mæviad," and his translation of " Juvenal."

Gifford—the meek, the mighty, honour'd dead !
I blame my breast that I no sooner read
Those noble pages,—each itself a roll,
Confirmatory of thy copious soul.—
    Great " Baviad," " Mæviad," arrows of satire,
(Than none but epicures can fail t' admire)
Which spread destruction, and set earth * on fire,—
And to oblivion hurl'd, like rats and mice,
Those who then dared to pamper forth their vice,
And made a trade by trafficking in rhyme,—
Display'd their trash, and hawk'd it as sublime !
    *   *   *   *   *

Proud is thy name, O Gifford !—but not I
Am equal to the task to laudify
So great a critic both of gods and men,
Who pounced upon them with thy able pen,—
Thus set them in the rank where each could boast
Of laurels won, or grieve of fortunes lost !
    No, no, dear Gifford,—mine is not the task
(And though thou 'rt gone—forgiveness I must ask)
To laud so great, so good † a man as thou ! * * *
Pardon me, friends ; and pray accept—my bow.

---

  * Those professing poets of the age, whom Gifford lashed with his peculiar wit and humour.

  † His munificence to the poor of his native town, in the form of an annual gift, will for ever revive the sacredness of his memory, thus :—Mr Gifford bequeathed property sufficient in value to realise the annual sum of £60 a-year ; £50 of which is equally divided among twenty poor persons of both sexes, and £10 is distributed in bread to other poor persons on Christmas Eve.

THE END.

www.ingramcontent.com/pod-product-compliance
Lightning Source LLC
Chambersburg PA
CBHW020355030726
47496CB00007B/2142